LORNA'S WAR

*To My lovely friend Julie
ENJOY!!
Lots of Love
Lynn x*

Lynn Riggs

authorHOUSE

AuthorHouse™ UK
1663 Liberty Drive
Bloomington, IN 47403 USA
www.authorhouse.co.uk
Phone: UK TFN: 0800 0148641 (Toll Free inside the UK)
UK Local: 02036 956322 (+44 20 3695 6322 from outside the UK)

© 2020 Lynn Riggs. All rights reserved.

No part of this book may be reproduced, stored in a retrieval system, or transmitted by any means without the written permission of the author.

Published by AuthorHouse 07/15/2020

ISBN: 978-1-7283-5464-4 (sc)
ISBN: 978-1-7283-5463-7 (e)

Print information available on the last page.

Any people depicted in stock imagery provided by Getty Images are models, and such images are being used for illustrative purposes only.
Certain stock imagery © Getty Images.

This book is printed on acid-free paper.

Because of the dynamic nature of the Internet, any web addresses or links contained in this book may have changed since publication and may no longer be valid. The views expressed in this work are solely those of the author and do not necessarily reflect the views of the publisher, and the publisher hereby disclaims any responsibility for them.

SYNOPSIS

Lorna Pashley lived with her mother and younger sister Maddie after fleeing from their abusive father.

Life was tough and money short but they felt safer than they had in a long time.

She didn't know it but her father would eventually find them but would he be the same man as he was before?

Lorna then met the love of her life Harry but with World War II on the horizon their life together would not be easy and when Harry went missing in action Lorna's life fell apart.

This is her story of how she survived not only her early years at the hands of her father who she was yet to meet again but the trials and tribulations of her life with and without Harry.

It is a story of one young girl's spirit to find happiness not only for herself but also for her beloved family.

THANK-YOU'S

There are several people I wish to thank for making this book come to fruition and there are a number more who I shall forget to mention so please accept my apologies and rest assured any help you have given is much appreciated.

I first must thank my wonderful husband Pete and son Michael for being there for me and supporting me in my absurd idea to write a book when I have never even written anything before. Talk about jumping in at the deep end!!!

Also to my sister-in-law Marie for her advice and guidance on medical matters which stopped me looking a prize wally!!

I would also like to thank Jenny Seale for her encouragement and introducing me to a local author Jacq Molloy who has given me lots of tips and writers knowledge.

Thanks also to Trevor Hughes who unfortunately passed away very suddenly who designed the wonderful book cover, such a talented individual and a great friend. It is such a shame that he didn't get to see the final printed version but I know that he is still with us in spirit and will see the result of his hard work. He is greatly missed by us all.

Thank you also to all my colleagues at Hawkes Farm Primary School for their encouragement and wanting to read the drivel I had composed once it was published!!

Finally my biggest thanks must go to my best mate Trish Luck who I sprung on her the fact I had written a book and would very much like her to be the first to read it. Her willingness to help edit the final draft was invaluable and I appreciate the huge amount of time she gave up to help me and made some very useful suggestions. I must also take this opportunity of thanking her Mum and Dad who pointed me in the right direction with regard to facts about the war years.

Thank you one and all and I hope that you enjoy the final story!!

This book is dedicated to my wonderful husband Pete and son Michael for their support in this venture and also to my best mate Trish Luck without whose support this novel would never have come about.
Love you all. X

CHAPTER ONE

It was a lovely spring morning in 1939 and Harry Weston had got up early to help his father get ready to load their boat with the day's consignment of coal for carriage from Birmingham to London along the Grand Union Canal.

Whilst Harry enjoyed the outdoor life it was not what he dreamt for himself as he had other ideas for the future that were more spiritual.

He had since his early childhood felt that he had a special gift to help people but being so young he could not explain it to the grown-ups and was only ridiculed as being "a bit peculiar". It was only his lovely old Nan that understood what he was trying to say and since she had passed away 8 years ago he felt totally alone and almost alienated.

Harry was now 16 and having just left school felt it was time to make a break and search out someone who understood and could help him develop this gift. That someone turned out to be Lorna Pashley who he met, quite by chance, at the local grocery store.

Lorna was the daughter of a dentist and Harry had always admired her from afar but today was tempted to speak to her as she was looking somewhat poorly and run-down.

His opportunity came when noticing her struggle as she was attempting to carry an overloaded bag of shopping to the door and subsequently dropping it all over the polished lino floor he went to her aid.

Harry bent down to help her pick up the items and in doing so brushed her hand. It was at that moment that a great tingle went through his hand and she gasped as she had the same feeling in hers which she had been suffering with for some time from terrible aches and swelling.

As if almost immediately the ache disappeared and upon looking up to see who was her knight in shining armour looked deep into the eyes of Harry and saw great compassion and love.

"Are you o.k." asked Harry, "You look to be having a bit of trouble there".

Lorna wanted to say yes everything was fine but what with her feeling so unwell and the troubles at home she felt that she could trust Harry and just wanted to have a friend she could blurt it all out to.

"I wish I could say yes but unfortunately that wouldn't be true" she replied. "Thank you for your help, you are an angel".

"My name is Harry and whilst I wouldn't normally say what I am going to say next, I feel that perhaps I can help you further. Do you fancy a quick cuppa next door at the Bellview when you have finished here?"

"Oh, thanks but I have a couple more errands to run, but if you can give me half an hour I could meet you there". Lorna replied.

"O.K" said Harry and he went to the till to pay for his groceries and both said goodbye with huge smiles on their faces.

Harry then went off back to their boat "Pelymi" with the shopping and since the boat was now fully loaded with goods for transit both him and his father had a couple of hours to spare before they needed to leave for London.

After a quick wash and change Harry went in search of his Dad.

"Just off for a quick cuppa with a friend" shouted Harry to his Dad who was tinkering with the engine down below. "Will be back in time for the off".

"No worries, have a nice break, this will keep me busy for a little while in any case" replied his Dad.

Harry then headed back to the Bellview and found a nice cosy table by the window. The Bellview was a lovely friendly café and was run by Bertha a huge cuddly lady who knew everyone and everything but was not in the least bit gossipy and was very confidential when anyone confided in her. She lived above the café in a small but elegant flat with her husband Fred and two cats Winston & Betty.

"Morning Harry love" she said as he entered and she came bustling over to serve him. "What can I get you today?"

"Just a cuppa for now Bertha, am meeting a friend in a minute so will have something more when she gets here".

"She???" Got a girly friend eh, anyone I know?"

"Bertha, you know everyone about here, but I am ashamed to say I didn't even ask her name. Met her a little while ago in the store, she was in a bit of a pickle and I helped her out. Agreed we would meet here for a quick cuppa after she ran a few chores".

"Been a knight in shining armour have we" replied Bertha. "You are a bit of an angel aren't you?"

"That's funny, cos that's what she said" laughed Harry.

A few minutes later Lorna rushed in looking somewhat flustered and out of breath.

"Hello Lorna love, my you look a bit out of sorts, take a seat and I'll bring you over a nice hot cuppa" said Bertha as she pottered about behind the counter.

Harry then waved from the table as Lorna was looking about and wondering if perhaps he had forgotten about their arrangement.

"So its Lorna then, felt so bad about not asking your name back at the store, are you o.k now, you are looking a bit hot and bothered?"

"Oh, it's been a bit of a nightmare and didn't think I was going to make it, why does everything go wrong when you are in a hurry?" she replied.

"Well, it happens like that sometimes, but you are here now and that's all that matters. Can I get you something to eat as I see Bertha has a cuppa on the way?" said Harry.

"A huge slice of that carrot cake would go down well" replied Lorna. "Bertha does bake the most gorgeous food".

"Well what a lovely compliment, I try my best" said Bertha as she approached with the tea. "I see you know each other, you sit down love and I'll bring over a piece of cake and a slice for your knight in shining armour here". She said with a twinkle in her eye.

Harry and Lorna then started chatting with Lorna first thanking Harry again for his help and then feeling that she could really open up to him despite not knowing him from Adam. She went on to explain that she had recently been suffering from severe aches and pains in her hands and hence dropping the shopping basket earlier but the strange thing was that when Harry brushed his hand against hers the ache completely disappeared.

Harry did not seem surprised at this as he had similar occurrences of this 'healing' gift before although he hadn't felt such a tingle as he had with Lorna.

Lorna felt very comfortable in Harry's presence and he seemed very open to listen to her about her life so she went on to tell him about the troubles at home and the stress related illnesses she had been enduring.

Lorna's father had been somewhat of a brute whilst she was growing up and whilst he had never laid a finger on her or her little sister he had taken out all his rage on their Mum who had kept quiet about the affair as she did not want to frighten her children. However, she and her sister Maddie would cower in the next room and try to blot out their mother's cries and screams as their Dad laid into her. This went on for a number of years before their mother had the courage to speak to her doctor and get some help. Needless to say it all came to a head one day when they all fled their home and relocated to another area.

They had been very fortunate that their Dad never had the desire to find them but it led to a lot of financial worries for them all with their mother having to work all hours which left Lorna to raise Maddie.

The stress was beginning to show as Lorna had just finished her last year at school and despite working hard she had left with no qualifications. However, she had no intention of ending up like her Mum firstly by being so dependent on a man and then being left as a single parent with no chance of securing a well-paid job.

Harry took this all in with great sympathy for Lorna and stressed his concern for her well-being and wanted to help in any way he could.

"I wish there was something I could do to help" said Harry

"I think you already have, not only does my hand feel better since you touched it earlier but I feel a great weight has been lifted off my shoulders by just telling you my troubles. I am so sorry if I have gone on a bit". "Now tell me about you, what deep and troubled past have you had?".

"Well, where shall I begin? Said Harry with a smile.

Harry then proceeded to relay his life story to a very interested Lorna. He told her about how he had lost his mother to cancer at an early age which hit his father really hard to the extent that he felt you couldn't live at their home any more due to the memories it contained and sold up and got a job transporting goods on the canal system. Having taken Harry with him they enjoyed a life of freedom and felt at one with the outdoor life. Over time the pain did ease but they both had times when some memories would surface over something minor which would make them both sad once more. Harry had tried to talk to his father about the gift he had but unfortunately his Dad did not believe 'in that sort of thing'. However, Lorna was taking a great interest in what he had to say and encouraged him to try and develop the gift and suggested going to see a friend of her mothers who gave readings on a regular basis at the spiritual church in the village.

The couple of hours they had to spare soon flew by and before they realised it was time to get back to work and

Lorna had to pick up her sister from school. They said some hasty goodbyes to each other and Bertha and rushed from the cafe with the promise that they would meet up again when Harry got back from London.

CHAPTER TWO

It seemed an age to Lorna waiting for Harry to return. Despite only having just met him it felt like they had been friends for years and she really missed talking to him, not only her problems but having a general chat about everything and nothing. Lorna didn't have many friends due to having to care for her little sister and help keep the house. She was also worried about her Mum who seemed to be getting more and more down about their situation and she knew that money was a main problem to them all.

She also knew that despite having left school, the small amount of money she brought in doing odd jobs for elderly neighbours was not really enough to get by on. She was actively looking for something better paid but without any qualifications she was finding it hard.

She was just on her way out to collect Maddie from a friends when her Mum came in a lot earlier than usual and when she asked why discovered that her Mum had been allowed home early as she was not feeling well.

"What's up Mum" enquired Lorna.

"Oh don't worry dear it's just that I have had this splitting headache all day that won't seem to shift. Think I will take some tablets and go to bed early if that's okay with you love. Are you able to give Maddie her tea and put her to bed?" replied her exhausted Mum.

"Of course Mum, you go and rest and I will pop up and see you when I get back with Maddie".

"Thanks love, you are such a help to me, just wish you didn't have to do so much. It's not a very nice life for you is it?" she said gratefully.

"My life is fine Mum, we all do our bit in this difficult time and it will get better I just know it".

"I hope so and thanks any way, see you later love" said Mum as she wearily climbed the stairs in their cosy little home.

Lorna was in heavy thought as she walked the mile or so to Maddie's friend's house and she really wished she had had the opportunity of talking with her Mum about the budding friendship that was developing with Harry and to ask her a bit more about her friend who worked at the church. She really wanted Harry to pursue the development of his gift and wouldn't mind going along with him.

Maddie was in good spirits when she got there and gloomy thoughts about her Mums health were pushed to the back of her mind in the hustle and bustle of getting her sister ready to leave.

It was dark when they got home and the house was in complete darkness when they approached which was very unusual as her Mum would always leave a light on somewhere. Lorna started to worry and rushed up the front path dragging Maddie behind her.

Once inside she rushed up the stairs to her Mums room and was immediately struck by the silence that met her. Normally there would be some sound of sleeping but there was nothing so Lorna rushed to her Mums side to try and wake her.

"Mum, Mum, please wake up" cried Lorna but there was no response. She was now very worried and quickly dashed outside to the phone box which was conveniently nearby to call for an ambulance. When they arrived a few minutes later and gave them a run down on her mother's health they informed her that they would need to take her to the hospital as her blood pressure was really low and was in danger of slipping into a coma.

"Can I just dash next door to see if they will babysit Maddie and come with you please" cried Lorna.

"Make it quick and we'll wait" replied the ambulance man.

After a short while she returned with their neighbour explained briefly to Maddie where they were going and not to worry they just wanted to check Mum over and then they would both be home. Also to be a good girl and do as Mrs Jeffrey's says and we'll see you when we get back.

The ride over to the hospital was short and bumpy and the speed they were going frightened Lorna even more. Oh please let her be alright prayed Lorna as she held her Mum's hand tight.

Once at the hospital everything happened so quick Lorna's mind was in a whirl and before she knew it she was sat beside her Mum's hospital bed looking down on her Mum who was connected to a gravity drip. Lorna was so glad that her Mum had been paying her shilling a week to the GP Scheme which covered them all for any medical expenses. She dreaded to think what this hospital visit and treatment would have cost them.

After what seemed like an age her Mum stirred which brought a nurse dashing over.

"Well Mrs Pashley that was a very close call you had there, how are you feeling?" asked the nurse.

"The pain seems to have eased, how long have I been here?" replied Lorna's Mum.

"Not long but it would have been quite a different story if your daughter had not come home when she did. How long have you been having these bad heads?" asked the nurse appearing very concerned.

"Oh a while now, they used to go with tablets but now they seem to stick around no matter what I take" she replied.

"That's because you have an infection that needs treating and if you hadn't become unconscious you would have ended up with a bleed on the brain and that could have been the end of everything. You need to take it really easy for a while and make sure you get enough rest".

"Easier said than done" replied Mum

"Mum you are to do as you are told, we'll get through this and Mrs Jeffrey has said she will help out, looking after Maddie and such, so you are not to worry" said Lorna who knew that it was up to her to take on more carer duties whilst her Mum was laid up but she was just grateful that her Mum was going to be ok now that they knew what the problem was.

Maddie was still up when she got home although she was snuggled up with Mrs Jeffrey on the sofa in a big fluffy blanket and was on the edge of sleep.

Lorna explained to her neighbour what had happened at the hospital and again her kindly neighbour reiterated that she would do everything she could to help.

"You are a real godsend Mrs Jeffrey, we don't know what we would do without you" said Lorna.

"Now don't you go worrying about anything love, I will call on you every day, get some groceries in for you and help with Maddie whenever you need me to. Oh and please stop calling me Mrs Jeffrey, it is so formal, my name is Isabelle and I am more than happy to help in any way I can. Now you get yourselves off to bed now and I will call round in the morning".

It was about 7 o'clock the next morning and true to her word Isabelle called round with a tray containing a full cooked breakfast, toast and milk for the girls. It was a Saturday and they had both planned on visiting the hospital to visit their Mum. Isabelle offered to drive them over which was a real help as the bus service on the weekend in their neck of the woods was not the most reliable or regular.

They arrived at the hospital a bit later to find Mum sitting up in her bed drinking a cup of tea. The doctor had just been round and was very pleased with her progress but stressed that she must continue with resting and taking it easy all the while she was taking the medication. On that basis he was happy for her to be discharged and made an appointment for her to return a week later for a check-up.

Both Lorna and Maddie were so pleased to have her back home and both promised the doctor that they would ensure that she didn't overdo it and that she had plenty of sleep and rest.

Isabelle who was waiting for them in the WRVS cafe within the hospital was also pleased to see them all and took them home and promised to drop some groceries in later that day.

It had been a long couple of days and it made Lorna wish all the more that Harry was back so she could have someone to talk to about it all.

No sooner had the thought left her mind than the front doorbell rang and she was thrilled to find Harry on the doorstep carrying a huge bunch of flowers with a huge grin on his face.

CHAPTER THREE

It was in a small town a few miles away, in a shady downtown pub that a fight was developing between a local patron and a visiting tourist. Both were in a very inebriated state and were fighting over the attention of the rather busty barmaid.

Minutes later the local police arrived on the scene and hauled both off for disturbance of the peace and to ascertain who the tourist was as very little identification was to be found on his person.

After spending a few sobering hours in a cold cell Arnold Pashley awoke feeling very sorry for himself and was wondering how he could have got into such a state. He was once considered to be a very respected dentist but since abandoning his wife and children nothing seems to have gone right. He had tried on numerous occasions to contact his wife for a reconciliation but was unable to find them. His own mother had no sympathy for him when he went to live with her for a while as it only confirmed what she had suspected in that he was beating up his wife but was confident that he hadn't touched the children. She really missed her grandchildren especially since she had lost her own husband a few years ago but whilst she felt that she could probably locate them she didn't want to do so as she was afraid that if Arnold found out then it would put them all back in danger.

Arnold now knew that he needed to get some help for this problem, not only for the drinking which seem to have escalated somewhat over the past few months but also for the rage that ensued from the effects of it. He knew his mother had lost patience with him and missed her grandchildren tremendously and this only made him feel even more guilty about the whole matter.

The only answer was to move well away and commit himself to some institution to sort it once and for all. He resigned himself to visiting his doctor once he got released from his current confinement and seek professional help.

Meanwhile back at No.7 Spilsdon Avenue, the home of Lorna, Maddie and their Mum Irene, Harry was sitting enjoying a nice cup of tea with them all and hearing about all the events of the past few days. He had got back from his London trip a couple of days earlier and been appraised of the situation by Bertha when he popped in with his Dad for a quick cuppa to the Bellview.

He was struck by his feelings of affection towards Lorna and really wanted to help her in any way he could. Having discussed it with his Dad he was encouraged to call round to visit her and see what he could do to help.

He was pleased to find them home when he rang the doorbell that early evening and was greeted with a huge smile on an otherwise very tired face.

"Oh Harry, how lovely to see you, please come in for a while" exclaimed Lorna

"Thank you, are you okay, have heard all about your troubles from Bertha at the Bellview, I'm so sorry to hear about your Mum, how is she doing?" replied Harry.

"Much better thank you, but she still needs lots of rest, here come through I'm sure she will want to meet you".

Harry followed her through the small but extremely neat hallway to a pretty front room which was very cosy and he immediately felt very at home.

"Mum, this is Harry that I was telling you about. He has just got back from London with his Dad" informed Lorna.

"Hello luv, please sit down, sorry I'm not looking my best but I'm sure you'll understand" replied Irene.

"Don't worry Mrs Pashley, I just called round to see if you are all okay. I don't mean to intrude but I must say I have missed Lorna since I have been gone and couldn't wait to visit any longer. Hope you don't mind me dropping in unannounced?" said Harry.

"Oh don't be silly, Lorna has told me all about you and rest assured she has missed you just as much. She also told me about the marvellous cure you gave her hand. Tell me do you have a natural gift for healing?" replied Irene.

"I don't know about that, have had one or two incidents when I was younger but since losing my grandmother have not really given it much thought as everyone I used to mention it to just made fun of me, it was only my grandmother that really understood" said Harry.

"Well I shouldn't take heed of what other people say, I have found that they only make fun because they don't understand or are afraid of such a gift" she replied. "Besides we all, in this family totally believe that there are some very special people put on this earth to help others and trust me I believe you are one of those very lucky souls, so I encourage you to develop your gift further".

"Thank you Mrs Pashley, since my grandmother passed away I have had no-one to whom I could talk to about this. I have always thought that I was here for a greater purpose but didn't have any idea how I could go about doing anything about it" replied Harry.

"Looks like you've come to the right place then. Why don't you join us next Saturday when we attend our Spiritualist Church meeting as I have a friend there who gives healing and I'm sure he will show you the ropes" explained Irene.

"Are you a healer yourself then?" enquired Harry.

"Oh, heavens above, no, but I wish I was. No, it's just that I go and see Frank so he can help me with the various aches and pains which I seem to get a lot of these days" said Irene.

"Oh, I see. Yes, I would love to come with you, it sounds just what I need" replied Harry.

At this point it was clear that Lorna's Mum was getting a bit tired so after a brief chat with Lorna in the hallway he made his excuses to leave as he didn't want to disturb her Mum but looked forward to meeting up with them on Saturday.

On his way back to "Pelymi" he gave the whole matter a lot of thought and was so pleased that he finally had someone he could talk to about this again and he felt with absolute certainty that not only could he help Lorna and her family but many others as well. He just needed to keep it from his Dad for the time being as he knew that he would only try and discourage him.

Meanwhile, back in the dingy jail cell Arnold was being processed for release on the proviso that he attends counselling for not only for his addiction to alcohol but also for his anger. He was given a name of a local therapist and whilst he initially baulked at the idea of seeing a 'shrink' he realised it would be the only way he could possibly turn his life around and perhaps if luck was on his side get his family back.

His first appointment was later that afternoon in an office directly behind the police station but he was at a loss as to what to do with himself till then. There wasn't time to go back to his Mum's so he decided to pop into a local cafe for a coffee to while away the time.

On the way he purchased a local paper for something to read to kill time whilst trying to make one coffee last the hour or so till he needed to leave.

It was there that he saw an advert for a Spiritualist Church that was holding a healing session for anyone that felt they needed it. It was a free event but all donations would be gratefully appreciated. Arnold almost laughed out loud as he thought the idea was total bunkum but as it was free he thought that perhaps there would be no harm in going along as it might help him with his current predicament.

So that's where he found himself some hours later after what he thought was a total waste of time at the therapist who spent more time delving into his childhood than anything else which he felt had no relevance on what was happening to him now. Still he had to keep up the sessions or he would land himself back inside which was not where he wanted to be.

Upon entering the church he immediately found himself uneasy as not only was he not a churchgoer but he didn't know anyone or what to expect. Needless to say he was greeted almost immediately by what seemed a frail old woman who he felt probably needed more healing than himself. She kindly introduced herself as Betty and welcomed him in and introduced him to the others that were already there.

Upon enquiring the reason for his attendance she allocated him to a young man called Roger Woodgate who she felt could help him. Arnold thought it very unlikely as he was so young and was immediately on the defensive thinking that there was no way this young chap could understand what he had been going through.

However, after about a half an hour of chatting Roger asked if Arnold wouldn't mind just closing his eyes whilst he placed his own hands upon his head. Arnold thought this a bit odd but went along with it and was immediately struck by how peaceful he suddenly felt. It was almost as if all his worries were lifted and he had some hope for the future. Perhaps there was something in all this baloney after all he thought.

After a few minutes, Roger removed his hands and asked Arnold to open his eyes.

"How do you feel?" asked Roger

"Well I have got to say that I came here somewhat of a sceptic but when you laid your hands on me I immediately felt a lot of peace" replied Arnold.

"That's because you have a lot of troubles bottled up in your head and heart and I tried to channel some healing to calm them. May I suggest that you come and see me on a regular basis as I sense there is a lot of anger and resentment that has built up over the years, some of which I feel could stem back to your childhood" stated Roger.

"That's funny you should say that as I went and saw a therapist earlier today and that was all he was interested in and I couldn't understand why. What has my childhood got to do with what I do now?" asked Arnold.

"Quite a lot actually, it has been known that history of behaviours can repeat themselves in off-spring and the way you were treated as a child can re-emerge in behaviours later in life. Also the history of our ancestors can be repeated in future generations. So if for example you had a great, great grandfather who showed a lot of anger then you could have inherited the gene that has brought it out in you" replied Roger.

"Oh, my Lord, I am in trouble then, please can you help me or am I a doomed case?" replied Arnold.

"No-one is doomed, it's just about healing the cause or inherited cause and finding peace with yourself and others. That I can help you with but you are going also to have to help yourself which can be done by talking to your therapist and answering any questions he may throw at you no matter how painful the memories might be" stressed Roger.

"O.K I will try and thank you so much for taking me on. I'm sorry but I do not have much money to give you for your time but please rest assured that it has been most appreciated" said Arnold.

"Don't worry about that, just give what you can afford, our payment is to see that we are doing some good in this world to heal those in need" replied Roger.

Arnold left the church feeling much lighter in spirit than he had for many years and couldn't wait to get back to tell his Mum all about it. He felt he needed her support if he was finally going to kick himself into gear and be a good person again.

CHAPTER FOUR

Saturday evening seemed to take forever to arrive and Lorna was excited to be seeing Harry again. It was also great that her Mum had taken to him so well and they had had a long chat after he had left which pleased Lorna no end as she did not often have the opportunity of having a heart to heart with her Mum, something she greatly missed.

Irene thought that Harry had a very strong gift for someone so young and that by coming with them on Saturday would give him the opportunity of developing it further. She was convinced that the ability was there which was evident from the instant relief her daughter had felt just on their hands brushing that time and she would support him in whatever way she could. She thought him to be a lovely young man with excellent manners and a very good heart and she certainly had no doubts if he wanted to take up with Lorna.

Harry arrived promptly at the agreed time and they all set off for the church in good spirits. Irene was welcomed with open arms as they had also got wind of her recent hospital stay and were all concerned as to her well-being. None more so than Frank who immediately wanted her to receive his healing in order to assist with any medication she may be on.

Firstly, though Irene insisted that he be introduced to Harry and after giving him a run-down on their short association left them to chat while she, Lorna & Maddie went over to have a cup of tea with a few of the others.

After a while Frank & Harry joined them and Frank relayed to them all about how impressed he was with Harry's untapped skill and whilst there was not much he could teach him he could help develop what Harry already knew to help him become an excellent healer. So much so he offered Harry the opportunity of joining their little group so he could sit in and observe the procedure they normally go through and if the public didn't mind, have a go himself.

Harry was well chuffed at this prospect and was so glad he had come along and couldn't thank Irene enough firstly for listening to him about it initially and then introducing him to Frank.

After a lovely evening, they all trotted off home and after Irene had taken Maddie upstairs to bed Harry & Lorna had a chat in front of the fire over a nice cup of cocoa. It was sometime later when they realised how late it was so they said their hurried goodbyes and held hands briefly at the door. It was at this point that Lorna again felt the relief in her hands which had started to ache again and said as much to Harry who also admitted that whilst his hands felt cool the palms were feeling very hot.

Harry got back to the boat quite late and his Dad had already retired for the night but had left him a note saying that he had hoped that he had had a nice evening and was looking forward to hearing all about it the following day.

The following day dawned bright and sunny, in fact a beautiful spring day full of hope and joy for Harry. He was first awake so he brewed a cup of tea and took one through to his Dad eager to tell him all about Lorna.

"Dad, wakey, wakey Have brought you a cuppa" said Harry

"Morning Son, that's a very welcome sight, did you have a good time last night?" replied Dad.

"Yes, it was great, I went and saw my new friend Lorna, she's a lovely girl and would love her to meet you" said Harry.

"Well you seem very taken with her so why don't you invite her over sometime, she sounds lovely" said Dad giving his son a quick wink.

"Thanks Dad, but we were talking that perhaps if the weather was good in a couple of weeks we could all go and have a picnic somewhere" replied Harry.

"WE?? Whose this royal we then?" asked Dad.

"Lorna, me, you and Lorna's Mum & sister. They are a lovely family and I'm sure you will like them" said Harry.

"Ooh it sounds pretty serious between you and this lass if the families are being introduced" joked Dad.

"Well let's just see how it goes shall we, no pressure!!" smirked Harry.

"O.K Sunday in a couple of weeks should be alright as we will be back from that short run to Braunston by then so perhaps we could get together in that lovely park round the corner from here?" said Dad.

"Brilliant, thanks Dad, I'll let them know. When are we heading off for Braunston?" asked Harry.

"This coming Wednesday, so should be back in plenty of time if the weather remains good" replied Dad.

They spent the rest of the day preparing the boat for the trip with Harry checking supplies and his Dad making some final alterations to the engine timing and clearing out the weed hatch. After that they all decided to go down to the local for a pie and a pint and perhaps a game of darts if a few of the other boaters were in.

In the meantime Lorna was up and about doing some chores whilst her Mum had a bit of a lie-in and no sooner had she finished and got Maddie up and dressed when there was a knock on the door. It was Frank calling round to speak to Lorna after being told that her Mum was still asleep.

"Hello, Lorna luv, glad to hear your Mum is doing as she is told and taking a much needed rest but actually it is you I wanted to speak to" said Frank

"Oh yes, why is that" thought Lorna, instantly worrying that he had picked up something from her Mum when he gave her healing yesterday.

"Oh nothing to worry about, was just calling by after meeting your friend yesterday.....Harry, wasn't it? It's just that he has such a remarkable talent and we have been advised of a seminar coming up later in the month for all spiritualist churches in the county and they have asked if there are any new members that might be interested and I thought Harry might like to come with me" replied Frank.

"Oh thank you, but I will have to ask him, how long is it for?" said Lorna.

"Only for a day, but it's a fairly early start which in his line of work shouldn't be a problem but was concerned how his Dad would take it as he told me that he didn't believe in 'all that stuff'" replied Frank.

"Oh I'm sure he can get away with some excuse providing he's not on a trip with his Dad" stated Lorna. "When do you need to know by?"

"Not till next week, it's just that they need to know numbers as they are laying on a bit of a spread etc for us" replied Frank.

"That should be okay. I expect to be seeing him before his next trip so will let you know, thanks so much for thinking of him" said Lorna.

"My pleasure, speak to you next week then" said Frank as he again wished her Mum & Maddie well and disappeared down the garden path.

Lorna was feeling on cloud nine right now as her life seemed to be taking a turn for the better, her Mum was getting better and hopefully with Harry's help could cure her of all her aches, pains and distress she had undergone recently. Whilst she was reluctant to ask him at such an early stage in their relationship it was nice to know that he would probably be more than happy to help if his past actions were anything to go by. Also her hands were feeling a lot better following his recent visit which she put down to his gift but was realistic enough to realise that probably her state of mind helped as well.

Irene finally appeared just before mid-day and found Lorna in the kitchen preparing lunch with the help of Maddie who had just asked if she could go to a friend's house to play that afternoon. Lorna told her to wait for Mum and ask her which when Irene appeared she went bounding up to to do just that.

It was agreed that she could and Lorna suggested it might be a nice walk for them all to drop her off and then they could go onto Bertha's cafe for a cup of tea as it was such a nice day. Irene welcomed the chance of a fully relaxing day and was so grateful to Lorna for everything she did and the long sleep this morning did her a world of good.

So that was the plan and they set off just after lunch to walk the mile or so along the canal towpath to Maddie's friend's house and agreeing to pick her up again just after 5pm.

They got to the Bellview Cafe just before 3pm and Bertha was so pleased to see Irene up and about and sat to chat and catch up with the budding romance of Lorna and Harry. Bertha made a complete fuss of Irene as was her wont to do as she knew how poorly she had been and the hard life she had previously led. They had been friends for many years now and Bertha was one of the closest friends Irene had and would often turn to her in times of trouble when the girls were small. Bertha was immensely proud of the way Lorna took care of things now and she deserved someone as nice as Harry in her life and she only wished she had thought of doing a bit of matchmaking earlier and get them together!!

Before they knew it and several cuppas later it was time to collect Maddie and make tracks for home so they said their fond goodbyes and set off. They were on the way back home with Maddie in high spirits as she had been asked to her friends birthday party to include a sleepover which she was very excited about and just as they were leaving the towpath Harry and his Dad came round the corner on their way to the local.

"Well fancy bumping into you" said Harry "Where are you off to?"

"Oh just been out for a walk to Bertha's and then picking Maddie up from a friends, just heading home now" replied Lorna.

"Sounds like you had a nice time.....oh by the way this is my Dad William......Dad, this is Lorna that I was telling you about and her delightful sister Maddie and lovely Mum Irene" said Harry.

"Pleased to meet you all, have heard so much about you from Harry here, he never stops talking about you all" replied William. "But please call me Bill, all my friends do and I can see where Lorna gets her beauty from."

"Oh pleeease" replied Irene, "It's so nice of you to say and nice to meet you too, Lorna has told me about the forthcoming picnic plan that she and Harry have been hatching up and really looking forward to it".

"Likewise, now that I have met you, I must admit I was a bit apprehensive when Harry first suggested it as I'm not normally one to get on well with strangers and didn't want to upset Harry as he is so taken with your daughter" replied Bill.

They went on to chat a bit more before Irene had to get the girls home for their tea but definite plans were made for the picnic in two weeks' time which they were all now looking forward to. After a gentle kiss on the cheek by Harry to Lorna they went their separate ways knowing full well that things were looking good for the future.

CHAPTER FIVE

Arnold was now attending his sixth session with the therapist and after many upsetting instances whereby childhood memories were almost too painful to tell the therapist about, it seemed to be getting to the bottom of the reasons for his anger and subsequent alcohol abuse.

He recommend a course of hypnotherapy to release these pent up emotions but also agreed with the spiritual healing that he had been receiving from Roger. The combination of the two seemed to be doing the trick and Arnold felt like he was making some progress. He hadn't been to the pub in three months and was surprised to admit he hadn't missed it.

His Mum was over the moon with the progress he had made and fully supported him both emotionally and financially. The therapist was costing a fair bit but she didn't mind if it meant that someday she would see her two gorgeous grand-daughters again. So she encouraged him every step of the way whilst harboring this secret hope and wishing all the while that it didn't all go pear shaped.

Arnold himself had made some secret enquiries as to their possible whereabouts but as yet no joy. Still he knew he still had a long way to go and was prepared to wait. In the meantime Roger, his healer was becoming a very good friend, despite their age gap he looked forward to the weekly sessions with him as he always came away feeling that little bit better about himself. Who knows one day I might be able to have the good life again that I lost so many years ago. He was certainly going to give it his best shot.

His next step was to get back to his old occupation but he knew that wouldn't be easy as his latest working record hadn't been good. He therefore made an appointment at his local hospital to see if he could help out in the dentistry department with a view to regaining some confidence and hopefully references in order to secure a paid position. It was either that or look to a complete career change but he had no idea as to what he would like to do or even what he was good at. Perhaps he would have a chat with Roger about it when he next saw him.

It soon came around for his next visit and after a successful session he asked if he might have a word about something.

"Certainly" said Roger, "Shall we pop along to the cafe down the road or do you wish to discuss it in a more private place?"

"No, the cafe will be fine, it's just that I would like your help with something" replied Arnold.

So they both strolled down to a local tea shop making polite conversation on the way.

"What's troubling you then?" said Roger once they had got settled at a corner table near the window.

"Well as my sessions with both you and my therapist have been going so well I have been thinking about trying to get back to work but as you can appreciate my latest track record has not been good. I thought of applying to the hospital but then perhaps a complete career change might be good but I have no idea what and was wondering if you could help" expressed Arnold.

"I am so pleased that you asked as I have been thinking how far you have come of late and I think that a new career path might be just what you need to boost your confidence" replied Roger. "Have you ever thought about work with the elderly? The reason I ask is that this church has a connection with a local old people's home and I know that they have recently lost their caretaker and are on the look-out for a replacement. The pay is not much but there is scope to build up some good references and perhaps in time you could utilise your dentistry skills to help out anyone that is in need".

"Oh, that sounds like a great idea, can you put a good word in for me?" replied Arnold.

"Surely can, I will mention it to my Mum later, she is one of the supervisors of the home and I know they will be grateful to find someone for the job" said Roger. "I will let you know next week if that's okay?".

They chatted for a further few minutes then went their separate ways. Arnold trotted off home to tell his own Mum the exciting news. He knew she would be very pleased for him as she had been supporting him all the way and they had discussed employment last night over tea. Arnold had been eternally grateful to her for not only putting him up in his hour of need but believing in him that he could learn something from his mistakes and make a better life for himself. She also knew of the home as she had an elderly friend live there before she had passed away last year and said it seemed to be a well-run place that respected their staff and patients alike and felt he would probably fit in well.

Arnold was feeling very optimistic about the future now and he soon received a call from Roger to say that he had arranged a meeting at the home for the following day at 11 a.m and to go along and ask for a Mrs Robertson.

So early next morning Arnold got up and spent some time getting ready (along with jotting down some questions he would like to ask) to ensure that he arrived promptly at The Paisley Retirement Centre as he wanted to set a good impression. He arrived about ten to eleven and was shown into a small but well organised office which was decorated with lots of plants and pictures of staff and residents both past and present on the walls. Mrs Robertson bustled in shortly after and welcomed him to the home and went on to explain what they were looking for and how desperate they were to find someone as there was no-one who could undertake the work and things were becoming a bit dire.

The conditions and pay seemed acceptable to Arnold and he had enough D.I.Y experience to handle what needed to be done which pleased Mrs Robertson no end. Also as he had been recommended by one of her supervisor's sons she felt quite happy to offer him the job there and then. It was decided that perhaps a tour round the home to meet the other staff and residents would be a good idea so off they went much to Arnold's delight that he could finally earn back some respect from the community.

In the meantime, Lorna had spoken to Harry about Frank's offer of the seminar and after checking with his Dad that they would not be on a trip was very pleased to accept. He still hadn't told his Dad yet of his dappling with the healing as he was still not sure he would let him continue so instead he just told him he was spending the day with Lorna. It was very exciting to start out on something new which he felt would be very successful for him and after much patience the end of the month arrived and he met Frank at the church so they could travel together as planned.

The day was a lovely sunny one although a slight chill in the air and the venue was in a lovely position by the river. Frank introduced him to all the people he knew there and they were soon sitting down to the first session of the day.

There seemed to be a lot of experienced people attending which made Harry feel that perhaps he shouldn't be there but Frank reassured him that this was just what he needed to develop his gift and that these people could help him with that.

There were several speakers initially that spoke of their discovery of spiritualism with some funny and heart felt anecdotes. However, whilst Harry found these very interesting and amusing he was anxious to sit in on the session that afternoon about healing. What struck him most from all the speakers that no matter how young or old they were they all had the same difficulty with accepting their gift and often had no-one to speak to of it for fear of ridicule. In all cases the only person they had would be a grand-mother or aunt but obviously they would often pass away before the individual could truly acknowledge the ability they had.

This gave Harry a great feeling of companionship with these strangers as the stories they told mirrored his own experiences and he said as much to Frank on the next break for refreshments.

"That is exactly why I brought you here" replied Frank "I felt that if you could hear these people it would make you feel like you were not alone in what you feel and give you the opportunity of not only speaking to them but to learn from them as they all have a lot to offer. Here let me introduce you to Belinda, I have known her for quite some time and she is a healer who started off much like yourself".

It turned out that Belinda lived in the next village and gave regular sessions at her house for people like Harry to develop their gift and when they were ready would take them to local nursing homes to help the elderly. Harry thought this a splendid and unpressurised way of developing his ability and said he would love to visit her to do that.

It was Belinda that was taking the session that afternoon and following her introduction she asked Harry to come up on stage for a demonstration. She explained to the audience that she had met Harry earlier that day and felt he would be an ideal candidate to show how to develop healing skills.

Harry was a bit nervous to say the least but Belinda soon put him at ease with her gentle easy going manner and was somewhat surprised when she asked another audience member who was suffering with some ailment to come up for Harry to practice on.

"But Belinda, I don't know how" exclaimed Harry.

"Don't worry, I will guide you through the process and from what you told me what happened with Lorna I think you will be surprised at how easy you are going to find this" replied Belinda.

What happened next was a complete surprise to Harry as Belinda had said. A gentleman had come up with severe pains in his elbow which despite medication from his doctor had not really solved the problem. Belinda asked the chap to relax in an easy chair that had been placed on the stage and with Harry sitting next to him she instructed Harry to close his eyes, gently hold the man's elbow in his hands and just imagine a blue light emanating from them over the man's elbow. The man immediately sensed a lovely warm heat direct at the point of pain and after about 5 minutes the pain just melted away. Harry by contrast felt his hands to be quite cool to the touch and was greatly surprised when he was told of this heat as he had not felt anything of the sort. Belinda went on to explain to them both that it was the transference of energy that had created this and it was quite usual to feel these effects. She knew that she had discovered something remarkable in Harry and was so pleased that Frank had introduced her to him.

The session ended soon after with such a huge round of applause it almost brought tears to Harry's eyes. There followed a general mingling session whereupon Harry found himself with a queue of people wanting to speak to him which he found somewhat overwhelming but very chuffed non-the-less. He couldn't wait to get back home and tell Lorna and her Mum all about it. What a day it had been and all from helping a beautiful young girl pick up her groceries!

CHAPTER SIX

It was Arnold's first day at the Paisley Retirement Centre and he was feeling a bit anxious as he had been out of work for a while and was not sure how he would cope. His fears, however, were completely unjustified as he was given a very warm welcome from Mrs Robertson as soon as he arrived.

After an initial cup of tea and a chat Mrs Robertson was almost apologetic to pass over to him a very long list of jobs that needed doing.

"They don't all need doing straight away" she said "But I have put them in order of importance so take as much time as you need, we are just so grateful to have someone here now that can undertake them".

Arnold checked the list and whilst quite lengthy some of the items would only take minutes to fix so it wasn't as daunting as he first thought.

"That shouldn't be a problem" replied Arnold "and I am equally grateful for you to giving me this chance".

"Oh don't be silly, I am sure you will fit in quite nicely here, do you want me to show you round again or are you okay" she replied.

"No, that's fine, I can manage" said Arnold as he got up to leave.

He was looking at the list again as he left her office and being totally engrossed in the tasks ahead didn't see one of the carers coming by with a tray full of used tea cups and bumped straight into her.

"Oh my gosh, I am so sorry" exclaimed Arnold as he bent down to help her pick up the luckily unbroken pieces of crockery. "What a chump I am, just wasn't looking where I was going" he continued as he looked into the most beautiful eyes that he had ever seen.

"That's o.k, no harm done. You're new here aren't you? Are you the new Caretaker?" enquired the petite tray carrier. "My name is Susan, but everyone calls me Sue".

"Pleased to meet you Sue, and yes I am the new Caretaker, Arnold's the name and can I say that you have the most beautiful eyes that I have ever seen".

"Oh don't you'll make me blush and get all in a fluster so I won't be able to carry these to the kitchen" she replied.

"Well then Sue, let me take them for you, just show me the way".

At that point Mrs Robertson who had heard the crash came dashing out of her office to see what the commotion was all about and was pleased to see that no-one was hurt.

"I see you have met our star carer then Arnold" said Mrs Robertson "You stick with her and you won't go far wrong" she said with a sly wink in Arnold's direction.

"Don't know what you mean Elsie" replied Sue "I'm just doing my job."

"And very well too, I just wish I could afford to pay you more, you are such an asset to this home" said Elsie.

"High praise indeed and I'll look forward to working with you" said Arnold.

"Well crack on guys and I'll see you both at this afternoon's music session, you will take time to join us won't you Arnold?" asked Elsie

"Oh, um... yes okay if that's alright" replied Arnold.

"Excellent, Sue will tell you all about it, see you later then" as she disappeared back into her office.

Sue went on to explain that every Monday afternoon there was a local primary school that sent their music teacher and a few pupils to the home to sing and play instruments for the residents. It was a hugely successful event which the residents thoroughly enjoyed as it gave them the opportunity for a good old sing-a-long or in the case of some of the older ones a chance to be lulled to sleep with the lovely tunes that the children sang out.

Arnold and Sue both then went their separate ways to undertake the various chores that needed to be done and agreed to meet up again at two o'clock in the main living room to enjoy the afternoon's entertainment.

The morning flew by and Arnold was engrossed in repairing one of the garden fences when he suddenly realised the time and went dashing indoors to clean up a bit. He didn't want to leave a trail of muck through the home as he could see how hard the carers worked in keeping it tidy.

He arrived in the living room just as the children were arriving so he took a seat next to Sue who had just finished dishing out cups of tea and plates of biscuits to everyone.

"This is the best time of the week" said Sue "All the residents are sorted and we get about an hour's peace just to relax and enjoy the time off".

"They look a contented bunch" replied Arnold "Have you been working here long?"

"Ooh about 6 years, I moved here from London after I lost my husband, I couldn't stand living with all the memories I saw there and London was getting far too busy for me, wanted a touch of the quieter life" replied Sue.

"Oh I'm sorry to hear about your husband, he couldn't have been very old" said Arnold.

"No he wasn't but his heart gave out from too much smoking, when they did an autopsy they found his lungs to be as black as a coal miners. I kept telling him to stop but he was very stubborn and wouldn't despite his health failing. He suffered a lot in the end so I guess it was a merciful release" explained Sue.

"I lost my wife too" said Arnold "Although she didn't die I just treated her and my girls very badly that understandably she left one day with them. I was in a very bad place back then and resorted to lots of bad habits which got me into trouble and eventually led to her divorcing me which didn't help. I eventually saw the light and got some serious help and this is the first job I have had since so I am hoping to gain back some self-respect and get a life back"

"That's so sad, especially when children are involved" replied Sue "Do you know where your family are?"

"No, have tried to find them but with no luck, I feel really bad for my Mum too as I know she misses her granddaughters something rotten but she wouldn't want to put them through any more aggravation like they used to get. I must admit I am very ashamed as to the way I was and it hurts me to think of all the wonderful things I had and threw away" said Arnold sadly.

It struck Arnold then that he had never been so open to someone so newly acquainted as he was and that he was suddenly afraid that Sue would think the worse of him for it. However, she seemed genuinely concerned about what he had been through and they went on to chat some more quietly whilst enjoying the music. She seemed to understand and commend him for getting help and pulling himself out of such a bad place and would help him in any way she could. She felt that doing the job he was now doing would give him back that self-respect as others are relying on him and she was sure that he would do an excellent job.

Arnold spent the following weeks and months tackling all the jobs on the list whilst at the same time building a wonderful friendship with Sue which had not gone unnoticed by Elsie and it was a bright summer's day when Arnold called into her office to inform her that all the jobs on the list had been completed.

"My word, so soon, well done, wasn't expecting that till later in the year" remarked Elsie "Will have to try and find you some more tasks to undertake."

"Well I have had an idea that I thought I would run past you if that's alright?" said Arnold.

"Fire away young man, what did you have in mind" replied Elsie.

"Well I was thinking that it is a shame that the beautiful gardens you have here aren't fully used, so I was thinking that perhaps a nice area paved with flag stones outside by the living room for the residents to sit and have tea would be nice. Also perhaps an area for the children to congregate for their Monday afternoon singing should the weather be nice" said Arnold. "It shouldn't take too much time to put together, I could get some costings if you like".

"Wow, that sounds like a splendid idea and as luck would have it we have now have some spare cash as I received a letter from a solicitor yesterday to say that a resident who passed away here a few months ago has had his estate settled and he has bequeathed us a tidy sum for making his last days so pleasurable. So yes, go ahead and get some quotes and I will have a look" replied Elsie.

Arnold spent the rest of the day doing just that and when he run the idea past Sue too, she thought it was an excellent idea and thought it would make better use of the super garden they had.

Meanwhile Harry had been continuing his tuition at Belinda's house who was happy for Lorna to come along too especially as Harry could practice on her hands and she was immensely proud at how far he had come in developing his talent. Lorna's hands were practically pain free now and she had developed a deep love for Harry but was too afraid to say how she felt although she was sure he had an inkling. Harry himself was feeling very confident in his ability, so much so that he had broached the subject with his father as he didn't want to keep it from him much longer as it was getting difficult making excuses now as to where he was going each time he had a healing session either at Belinda's or a meeting. Bill was shocked at first that he was dabbling in such rubbish but when he spoke to Lorna and saw the difference Harry had made to her he figured that perhaps there was something in this malarkey after all.

Harry really wanted him to come along to one of the meetings to see him in action but felt that perhaps he wasn't quite ready for that yet. Still one day he will realise that I have this gift and be proud imagined Harry.

Needless to say that opportunity came sooner than he thought and it was one summers evening when they were on the final stage of their trip back from London after delivering a load of coal that Bill took a leap from the boat to set the next lock and misjudged the gap and came crashing down onto a lump of rock which was just below the surface of the water. He felt his knee twist and a horrendous pain shot up and down his leg.

Harry managed to moor up and pull his Dad from the water to find that his left leg at a very peculiar angle. So he made him as comfortable as he could and dashed off to the nearest telephone box to call for an ambulance.

It was a short while later that the ambulance arrived and carefully loaded Bill on a stretcher and carried him along the towpath to the nearest road and the waiting ambulance. Harry had grabbed some bits and thrown them into a bag and went with him, hoping that it wasn't a broken kneecap or anything else too drastic.

They were still at hospital sometime later, Bill had been put in a bed and the doctor came on his round and approached Bill with an x-ray in his hands.

"I'm afraid we are going to have to operate Mr Weston, you have smashed your knee cap and we need to put a plate in in order to piece the broken bone back together. It means you are going to be in a cast for a couple of months as it needs to be kept immobile" stated the doctor. "We will get you down to the operating theatre as soon as possible but there may be a bit of a wait, I will get the nurse to bring you some painkillers in the meantime okay?"

"Yes, doctor, thank you. Do you know when I will be able to get back to work?" replied Bill.

"Let's see, I see from your notes that you work the boats, is that right?" Bill nodded. "Well as I say you will be in a cast for a couple of months and then there will be some physiotherapy needed so not in the near future I'm afraid" replied the doctor.

With that he was called by a nurse to another patient who was creating a fuss at the other end of the ward.

"Dad why don't you let me try and help you, you can still go down for the operation but I might be able to ease the pain in the meantime" said Harry.

"Alright son, give it a go, you know how I hate taking tablets so I've nothing to lose have I" he said in a joking sort of way.

Harry quickly pulled the curtain round his Dad's bed and asked him to lie still and quiet and to just relax as much as he could. He then proceeded to lay both his hands on his Dad's knee and imagine a blue light around them just as he had been taught and allowing the energy to flow. His Dad suddenly gasped as he felt the heat from his son's hands giving out such a penetrating warmth which instantly dulled the pain he felt. He continued to lie still not quite believing that this was happening and suddenly realising that perhaps his son had this extraordinary gift after all.

It was a short while later that the nurse called by to say that a slot had come up in the theatre and they were ready to take him down for his operation. Harry said he would wait for him in the nearby corridor which had been furnished with a few hard chairs for relatives to wait out in suspense. The nurse said someone would fetch him once he was in recovery.

During this time Harry took the opportunity of calling Lorna on her neighbours phone to explain what had happened and that it would be unlikely that he would be able to come and see her tonight as planned but would keep her posted as to what was happening. Lorna thanked him for letting her know and asked to pass on her good wishes to his Dad and would be thinking of him.

No sooner had Harry returned to the lounge a pretty young nurse came to tell him that his father was out of the operating theatre and back on the ward if you would like to go up. When he got there the surgeon was with him and was eager to speak to Harry as his Dad was still a bit groggy from the op.

"How did it go?" enquired Harry.

"Well I have to say I have never seen anything so remarkable in all my career" replied the surgeon. "We had the x-ray of your father's knee which was pretty smashed up I have to say, but when we opened it up all we found was a hairline fracture. I really don't know how that happened, I'm guessing that the x-rays have somehow got mixed up which doesn't seem possible as we have had no other admissions for knee problems"

"Does that mean he won't need to be in a cast for two months then?" replied Harry.

"Just six weeks will probably be enough" said the surgeon "But come back after three and we will have another look at it".

"That's great news, thank you" replied Harry knowing full well that the x-ray was the correct one but the bit of healing that he had given his Dad was powerful enough to mend a lot of the damage.

Harry then pulled the curtain back round his Dad's bed thinking if he had done that much good the first time hopefully he can try again with the hope that any healing could penetrate the plaster cast on his Dad's leg and help some more. It was during this healing session that his Dad came round fully from the anaesthetic and Harry told him what the surgeon had said. His Dad admitted that he was not surprised as he had felt such a relief from his son's hands but he didn't realise how much benefit it had been. He promised never to belittle his son's ability again and now had a total change of mind as to the power of healing and was no longer a sceptic.

Harry was overjoyed that he now no longer had to hide this from his Dad and was immensely pleased that he could help in his recovery.

CHAPTER SEVEN

Lorna and Harry's lives moved along at a steady pace with them becoming closer every day. Harry and his father had given up working the boats as his Dad was now finding his knee giving him a few twinges when jumping on and off the boat. Harry's healing had had a remarkable effect and was indeed healed completely in the three weeks. Bill got a job locally at the coal merchants following a contact he had made whilst hauling coal and the position came with a lovely little cottage which was just right for them both.

Harry carried on with his healing work which earnt him a little money but he felt that if he was to support Lorna in years to come then he needed to have a secure job. Not sure what he wanted to do he joined his father at the coal merchants in the office processing all the orders and ensuring that payments were up to date. Not exactly exciting work he thought but the pay was good and he was planning on asking Lorna to marry him as he loved her dearly and his Dad thought the world of her.

It was with this in mind that he was running through how to go about it when he wandered home one Friday night from work to find is Dad already home when he opened the door. He looked ashen faced and when he asked him what was wrong his Dad handed him a buff coloured envelope which they both knew what it contained without even opening it.

Harry had turned 18 earlier that year and England was in the full throws of war with Germany and as suspected Harry had just received his call-up papers and was to report to the local army barracks the following Monday. His Dad was distraught at the prospect as Harry was the only family he had left and to lose him as well as his wife seemed unthinkable. Harry tried to reassure his Dad that it would be okay, but was anxious to go and see Lorna with his proposal as time was now very limited.

He quickly put the letter in his pocket along with the engagement ring that had belonged to his much loved mother knowing that she would want him to give it to whoever he decided to marry.

The ring was beautiful, set with a lovely blue sapphire in a cluster surrounded by tiny diamonds. Harry's Dad had saved several months wages to buy it for his Mum and Harry had always admired how it sparkled on her finger. He tried hard to compose himself whilst he headed over to Lorna's so she didn't suspect anything was wrong. He was hoping that she would like it as it would please his Dad for it to become somewhat of a family heirloom and had given it to Harry with his blessing along with the plain wedding band that she had also worn.

He arrived shortly after six o'clock and rang the bell which was opened by Maddie who adored Harry like a big brother and was a great male influence on her since she didn't remember her father due to them all fleeing for their safety a number of years ago.

Lorna came down the stairs shortly after and was surprised to find Harry in the hall and after a brief excuse as to why he was there she donned on a light jacket to go for a walk. Harry was a bit quiet and she was concerned that something was up but Harry just said that there was something he needed to ask her and could they go to the park and have a chat.

Once they got there they sat down on their favourite bench which was in the prettiest part of the park and was a favourite spot for both of them. Harry seemed a bit hesitant about how to proceed and break both good news and bad at the same time.

"What's up love, you seem very worried about something?" said Lorna

"I don't know how to say this" said Harry and Lorna was instantly worried that what she knew would eventually happen was now the case. "You know how much I love you, don't you Lorna?" he said. "Well over these past few months I have felt that life without you would not be worth living.... and....well......what I'm trying to say is......will you marry me?" he stumbled as he produced the small velvet covered box from his pocket and opened it for her to see.

"Oh Harry, I have been waiting so long for this moment but wasn't sure how you felt and yes, the answer's YES. I love you so much and the ring it's beautiful" replied Lorna as she slipped it on her finger. It was a size too large but Harry said that they could take it to a local jeweller for it to be resized. Lorna felt very honoured to be given something of such sentimental value and vowed to keep it safe at all times. His father obviously had great taste in jewellry after Harry had told her the background to the ring.

After a long embrace and passionate kiss they parted and Lorna looked with concern at Harry as he seemed to have something more on his mind.

"There's something else isn't there?" she asked.

"Yes, yes I'm afraid there is" as he pulled the envelope from his pocket. Lorna didn't need to know what it said as she already knew and had been dreading this moment since he had turned 18.

"How long have we got?" she asked almost tearful now.

"I have to report at the barracks on Monday" Harry replied. "They will then give me two weeks solid training and will then be shipped to join 25 Regiment of the Royal Artillery in Germany. I am not allowed any leave or visitors before I go so we only have this weekend left".

Lorna couldn't hold back the tears now and Harry had difficulty whilst he hugged her tight and walked her home. It was going to be equally devastating to tell her Mum and sister who were both very fond of him. They had all grown very close over the past couple of years and Harry considered them to be family even now. This was a very depressing time for them all.

"Please will you promise me something" said Lorna as they neared home. "Please don't be a hero and keep safe for us".

"I don't plan on doing anything dangerous but unfortunately it's not up to me but I will do as best I can. I don't want to go, it's going to tear me up to be away from you" he replied.

"I'll write every day but I understand that it will be difficult for your to write back but just know that I will always be thinking of you and I shall look at the moon each night knowing that you are looking at it too" said Lorna in between sobs.

They finished the rest of the walk in deep silence each with their own troubled thoughts and when they arrived home and Irene saw the look on their faces she somehow knew what it was about.

They tried to cheer up a bit and told her of their engagement which thrilled Irene no end and she was very happy for them it was such a shame that the joy was marred by Harry's impending call-up.

The rest of the weekend was spent trying to live each and every minute to the full but all too soon Sunday evening rolled round and Harry had to leave Lorna and go home.

As they had their final hug and passionate embrace on the doorstep Lorna just broke down and clung to Harry all the more.

"Please stay safe my love and come home to me again soon" she sobbed and it broke Harry's heart to leave her like that but promised to write as often as he could.

Irene came to the door and gently prised Lorna off him and telling him also to stay safe and that Lorna will be o.k and not to worry about her and just make sure he comes home again soon. Harry left for home then after thanking Irene and to give his love to Maddie who had not been told the news yet as he loved that little girl too and didn't want to upset her. Irene said she would explain it to her soon as she was sure to want to know as soon as she saw Lorna so upset.

Harry got home to find his Dad with red eyes as if he had been crying which he denied of course but Harry knew it was equally hard on him as he always feared the worse. Whilst he knew that if anything happened to him Irene would look after him as they had become quite close too it didn't help to leave him feeling so alone.

"It will be alright Dad" he said. "Irene and the girls are always there for you, you know"

"I know son, don't take no notice, I'm just being a bit daft that's all. Here let me go and put the kettle on and we'll have a bit of supper" he replied.

They spent the rest of the evening chatting quite late into the night before Harry went to bed feeling very apprehensive about what the future was to bring. This should have been a joyful time now that Lorna had agreed to become his wife but that felt completely overshadowed now. Still, he thought, he was still glad he had asked her as it was something to hang onto whilst they were apart.

The following day dawned overcast and rainy which seemed to reflect just how he was feeling but he made his way as instructed to the local army barracks and was amazed to find many other young men like himself queued up to register. Whilst some were eager to get going and show the Jerries what they were up against there were a few like Harry who felt distraught and being torn from their family and loved ones to fight for what seemed to them not their business.

Army life turned out to be very harsh and the regime imposed very difficult to get used to. Harry did his best to learn what was required not for the benefit of the army but just to ensure that he could keep himself as safe as possible in order to keep his promise to Lorna and her family.

He had already received two letters from Lorna which she tried to keep up beat and telling him all that she was doing but she always ended the letters in the same way *"I'll always love you so please don't be a hero and I'll see you with the moon tonight".* He always looked at the moon wherever he was and it somehow made him feel closer to her and he hoped she felt the same.

The training was vigorous and concentrated and all too soon it was time to leave, not for Germany as originally advised but to France where fierce battling had been going on. Harry had managed to get two letters out, one to Lorna and one to his Dad advising that the original destination had changed and unfortunately he was not allowed to tell them where they were heading but asked them both to pray for his safe return.

Lorna was quite distraught when she received the letter as she had been following developments on the radio and knew the area he was going to was most dangerous. She had been with her mother and sister to the Spiritualist church every day to pray and had asked Frank if he could see anything untoward in the future using the skills of a medium. She suspected that even if he had seen anything bad he would not have told them as he didn't want to dampen their spirits, all he would say was that their angels will look after them but they must ask for their help as they cannot intervene without it. Lorna went straight home and wrote to Harry relaying this message and praying that he got it in time.

Time was quickly passing and whilst it seemed to drag for Lorna, it was soon approaching the first Christmas without Harry, it would be awful this year and she had visited Harry's Dad insisting that he spent Christmas with them. She didn't want him to be on his own and it seemed only right that as he was to be part of the family that it should start now. Bill wasn't sure at first but Irene wouldn't have it any other way and made up a spare bed in the front room so he could stay and they could all be together at this difficult time.

Christmas came and went and Bill stayed on for a few more days till he had to go back to work. Both Lorna & Bill felt it very hard to keep their spirits up but made their best efforts for the sake of Maddie and Irene. They had spent most evenings glued to the reports on the wireless and praying together to keep Harry safe. Neither he nor Lorna had received any letters in weeks and they were getting worried but when they made enquires at the barracks they were told that no mail shipments were being made as all resources were being used to ship troops. So they just had to hope and pray even more that no harm had become him and carry on as best they could.

The new year of 1942 dawned with still no word from Harry, both Lorna and Bill had made enquiries but they knew what the answer was to be as they had been listening to the reports on the radio and were aware of how bad the fighting had been in Europe. The bombings in London had also been reported on and Irene was so glad that they didn't have that to contend with too. Needless to say Lorna made another trip to the barracks in the slim hope of some letter no matter how short from Harry would be waiting for her.

The soldiers had got to know her well from her regular visits and this time as she walked up the road a young cadet ran up to her with two letters in his hand. One was for her and one for Bill. After thanking the young lad she ripped hers open immediately right where she stood and with tears in her eyes read the all too short, hastily scribbled words from her beloved. It didn't say too much and due to security

Harry couldn't say where they were stationed but he assured her that he was doing everything possible to keep safe and meeting her on the moon each night.

Lorna then run as fast as her feet could carry her to his Dad's house to deliver the other letter and waited in anticipation and watching Bill's face very closely as he read the letter. She immediately sensed his relief as she herself had felt that Harry was okay and whilst his Dad's letter didn't say much either they both felt they could celebrate a little.

Life continued much on the same vein with regular trips to the barracks for word from Harry to no avail and they continued to pray for his safety. Bill came over every Sunday for dinner and they would listen to the radio for the latest updates which weren't looking too good but they all tried not to worry.

Lorna continued to talk to Harry via the moon each night before she went to bed and she knew that wherever Harry was he would be doing so too. This gave her a little comfort and helped see her through the next day.

Winter soon turned to spring and the days were warmer which helped with everyones spirits. Lorna had left school some months before and was helping out Bertha at the Bellview, which, whilst she enjoyed serving and chatting to the customers, she felt that perhaps she should be doing something more to help with the war effort and all the brave soldiers that were putting their lives on the line for King and country.

It was with this in mind that she made enquiries as to whether there was any work she could undertake to help. However, having just turned 19 she was still too young to be enlisted. They informed her that she could join the

Auxiliary Territorial Service as soon as she was 20 but until then they were sorry but they couldn't help. They were very apologetic as they were very anxious to employ someone who was that keen. She promised that she would call back on her birthday next year but was secretly hoping that the war would be over by then and she would have Harry back in her arms.

CHAPTER EIGHT

Arnold's time at the Retirement Centre was becoming increasingly enjoyable, he was earning himself a good reputation for being reliable and conscientious and his friendship with Sue was going exceedingly well.

He had undertaken a number of more substantial projects much to the delight of Elsie who couldn't praise him highly enough to any visitor that called at the home. She had also noticed the developing friendship he had with Sue of which she was also glad as she often felt that Sue had been quite lonely since moving from London following the loss of her husband a number of years before. Elsie was secretly hoping that an engagement was on the horizon as both her and the residents of the home would welcome a bit of good news and celebration in these dark times of war.

"Oh well, onto business", she thought, "I can't spend all day day-dreaming about things that might not be" as she opened the days post which had recently been brought in by one of the carers.

One of the first letters she opened was about their regular visits from local primary schools, it was a request from a school in a small town not far away who had heard of the visits they had and would like to take part in a similar visit as the Head Master thought it would be a good idea for the children to visit other towns by way of a geography field trip and a music lesson all in one. He was wondering if a date could be arranged at their convenience and would welcome a visit to see her perhaps next week.

The visits by the school had always been a success so Elsie wrote back welcoming the idea and perhaps he could undertake a preliminary visit the following Wednesday. It would be helpful if he could bring with him a list of the children's names that would be attending the sing-a-long as she liked to memorise them beforehand so she could learn them and associate them to faces when they arrived.

The following Wednesday a very smart and proper gentlemen called at the home to see Elsie as previously arranged.

"Good morning Mrs Robertson" he said in a very refined manner. "My name is Ron Deeley and I am the Head Master of Falcon House Primary School and it's a pleasure to meet you".

"And to you Mr Deeley, please come into my office and we can discuss matters further" replied Elsie.

They wandered into her office and she showed him the comfy chair so they could sit and have a relaxed conversation.

"I understand that you wish for a selection of your pupils to come and visit us for a music recital" said Elsie.

"Yes, that's right, we have heard such good reports from Hairbourne School at how well it has benefited the pupils and we would like to be involved with the scheme also if that is o.k with your good-selves" replied Ron.

"It's so good to hear that the pupils enjoy it, we have had Hairbourne School visiting us for a number of years now and the residents thoroughly enjoy the event so we would more than welcome you to our home" replied Elsie. "How does a Friday morning, about 10.30 suit you?".

"That sounds splendid, but I will need to check with our music teacher Miss Porter and perhaps I could let you know" said Ron.

"Good, that's settled then, just let me know which week you would like to commence the visits and I will make arrangements with the carer's to ensure that everyone is present in the lounge area" said Elsie

"Did you bring the list of children's names with you?".

"Oh yes, here it is, there will only be about 10 to start with but that may grow in time if that is o.k with you" replied Ron.

"The more the merrier!" joked Elsie as she perused the list that he had handed to her.

Immediately one name sprang out at her, Madeline Pashley!

"Oh my word", she thought to herself as she showed Mr Deeley out after thanking him for his time and that she looked forward to seeing either himself or Miss Porter with the children soon and went back into her office wondering what to do about the possibility of this young girl being Arnold's daughter.

Elsie had been made aware of the history behind Arnold coming to her for work all that time ago and she knew how desperately he had been to find his family but she also knew that it was not her place to intervene as it could create a lot of upset.

She thought it might be a good idea to wait until the children visited to see if he recognised her, although

Madeline had been a toddler when she had last seen her Dad and would no doubt not remember him at all. In the meantime she would have to keep the list out of sight as she didn't want to alert Arnold unnecessarily.

However, the thought played constantly on her mind so she called Sue into her office later that afternoon and showed her the list.

Sue, who had become extremely close to Arnold immediately spotted the same name and came to the same conclusion.

"Oh, my goodness, what shall we do?" she asked Elsie.

"I'm not sure, that's why I called you in here. I know you are aware of what happened in his family and I am sure that they are quite settled in the knowledge that they are safe and free of him, but he has changed so much from what I gather and I know he is desperate to find them even if it is just to say that he was so sorry" replied Elsie.

She went onto explain that her initial thoughts were to wait for the recital to take place and see if he recognised her, which she was confident he would, although Madeline would not know him being so young when they left. This Sue agreed was a good idea and that she would talk to Arnold straight after the recital to discuss what to do next as she was also sure that Arnold would recognise her.

It was therefore the following Friday that both Mr Deeley and Miss Porter piled onto the bus with the children and headed for the Retirement Centre. The children were all very excited at the prospect of a morning out of school and were in good spirits and sang the whole way there.

They arrived just before half past ten and were shown onto the paved terrace as the weather was very warm for late

Lorna's War

spring and the home was making full use of this marvellous facility that Arnold had built some time ago.

They were in their first rendition of 'White Cliffs of Dover' that Arnold came out with Sue and a couple of trays of tea for the residents. After distributing them amongst the audience they both took a seat at the back to watch the performance.

Arnold suddenly grabbed Sue's hand and pulled her to her feet, dragging her inside with him.

"It's her, it's her" he shouted.

"Who?" replied Sue knowing all too well what she expected would happen.

"It's Maddie, I swear it's Maddie" he was almost crying now with the thought that he may have finally found his family.

"I think we had better go and see Elsie" said Sue, she will have all the names of the children and may be able to find out more for you".

They both hurried off in search of Elsie who was also expecting a knock on her door at any moment.

"Come in" she called.

"Elsie, can we speak to you for a moment please?" said Arnold excitedly.

"Of course, what appears to be the problem?" she replied, knowing all too well what was about to come.

"I believe you have a list of all the children's names that are performing today and I wondered if any of them is called Madeline Pashley" he asked somewhat expectantly.

"Now Arnold, I don't want to get your hopes up here but when the Head Master came to see me initially and handed me the list I did notice the name but didn't want to mention it in case it wasn't your daughter as that would have been an awful disappointment to you. You obviously recognise the young lass but equally do not wish to frighten the young girl as I don't know what she has been told about you. I will, however endeavour to contact her mother and explain the situation but please be prepared that a reconciliation may take some time, if ever" replied Elsie.

"I know it's her, I know it's her" he repeated "Please can you do everything you can to help me here, I will be most grateful".

"Of course I will Arnold but just for now go back and enjoy the rest of the morning and don't mention anything to her until I have spoken to her mother.... Irene, isn't it?" Elsie asked.

"Yes, that's right and I promise not to say anything untoward" replied Arnold hardly able to contain his excitement.

They both then went back onto the terrace and Sue had her hands full to keep him quiet whilst the children were singing their melody of songs but he didn't once take his eyes off the pretty young girl in the second row who without a doubt meant so much to him.

After the school had left, Arnold couldn't have had a bigger smile on his face if he tried but Sue was a little unsure about what was to follow because if his ex-wife refused for Maddie to see him she knew he would be devastated.

Meanwhile Elsie was trying to work out how the best way to approach Irene and felt that a phone call or letter would be too impersonal so she decided to visit the school and speak with Mr Deeley who if he was agreeable could arrange for Irene to be there too.

So that is what happened, the following week Elsie hopped on a bus to school and at the appointed time was sitting in Mr Deeley's secretary's office waiting for him to speak to Irene in his own office and explain who he was about to introduce her to.

Irene had previously received a letter from Maddie's Head Master who had asked her to call in to discuss a matter relating to Maddie. She was immediately worried that she wasn't doing well at school which surprised her somewhat as Maddie had always enjoyed school and had many friends which was a great comfort to her. Lorna had told her not to worry that it was surely something quite the opposite to what she imagined and just to go along and see what it was about. Lorna had offered to go with her but she knew that Bertha was relying on her at the cafe so told her that she would be fine.

Irene promptly arrived at the school at the appointed time and was welcomed by Mr Deeley and asked to take a seat in his office.

"Thank you very much for coming Mrs Pashley" said Ron. "I know this must have come as a bit of a surprise to you but we have had an unusual situation occur which involves Maddie. Don't worry she hasn't done anything wrong, in fact quite the opposite, she is a model pupil and we are very proud how she has progressed since she has been with us".

Irene breathed a sigh of relief but couldn't help but wonder what on earth could have happened to make it so important to bring her into school.

"I would first like to introduce you to a Mrs Robertson who runs a Retirement Centre in the next town" said Ron who arranged for Elsie to be brought through. "Now you are obviously wondering what this has to do with Maddie and I would like Mrs Robertson to explain"

Elsie who had been brought in at this point didn't quite know where to start so she just went back to the beginning in the hope that what she was about to tell Irene would not distress her too much.

"Well as you know Maddie visited our home recently with her school for a music recital and I must say that we were very impressed with all the children's lovely voices" she said. "However.... prior to that Mr Deeley here kindly provided me with a list of names of the children as I like to get to know them as it makes it more relaxing for them…I hope you understand" she continued.

"It was from this list that I spotted your daughter's name which is the same as our caretaker's and wondered if there were any relation" said Elsie.

It was at this point that Irene's heart sank and all the colour drained from her face. She knew what Elsie was going to say next and what she had been hoping and praying wouldn't happen was about to come about.

Elsie continued,

"His name is Arnold and has been with us for some time now and I am fully aware of his history and the trouble he has been in. However, since he has been with us he has been a godsend and is currently in a relationship with one of our top carer's who speaks very highly of him and also knows of his background".

"He has never laid a finger on anyone in the home and has been having therapy for his previous troubles which has had a remarkable effect" said Elsie. "Now as you might have guessed he recognised Maddie when she came with the school and came to me for help in arranging a meeting with you all as he has been desperately trying to find you of late".

Irene was now feeling quite faint at the thought that she hadn't escaped him after all and Ron noticed how pale she had become and arranged for a glass of water to be brought to her.

"If I might interject here" he said. "It sounds like your ex-husband has turned his life around and is desperately sorry for what he has done. He seems also to be in a secure relationship with this other lady who along with Mrs Robertson speak very highly of what he has achieved".

"We would not normally get involved in marital issues but in view of knowing you and both you daughters I would like to offer whatever help I can, perhaps if Mr Pashley wanted to come here with his friend from the home and you could bring the girls, we could be with you in case any problems occur. We would of course be happy to give you some privacy if you wished here in my office".

It was at this point that Elsie reached across and took Irene's hand.

"My dear, I know how difficult this must be for you but please believe me when I say that I do not think Arnold is now the man that you were married to and it has been tearing him apart at how he treated you and the girls, he is so sorry that he didn't get help sooner. He is not expecting you to forgive him and he doesn't expect you to take him back, he just wants to be friends and have some sort of father/daughter relationship again with his girls" said Elsie.

Irene thought for a moment and decided that this was not a decision she could make on her own and that she desperately needed to talk to Lorna about it. She therefore thanked Elsie for what she had told her and explained that whilst she was initially shocked to the core that they had been found she appreciated what she had said but needed to talk to her daughters about it. Maddie obviously had no idea who he was as she had been so young when they had fled to safety so this was going to come as a big shock to her.

She promised to keep in touch with Elsie and Ron and was very grateful for any help they could give, this was going to be a difficult time and not one she was looking forward to at all.

CHAPTER NINE

Lorna arrived home later that day after a very busy shift at the cafe, Bertha was relying on her quite a bit but she loved all the interaction between the customers who were a jolly bunch and always asked after her and her family.

She was surprised when she opened the door to the silence that met her as usually there was a radio on and the smell of dinner cooking, but today there were none of those things and she was immediately worried that something had happened to her Mum.

"Mum, are you here?" Lorna called out.

"In the front room love" Irene replied.

Lorna popped her head round the door and was surprised to see her Mum all ashen faced and with red eyes as if she had been crying.

"Whatever's the matter?" asked Lorna instantly worried that perhaps she had received some bad news about Harry. "What's happened Mum, was it something bad about Maddie at school today?".

"No, Maddie is fine, quite a star pupil as it turns out" she replied.

"Then what's up to get you so upset?" enquired Lorna.

Irene went on to tell Lorna of the day's events and how their father had finally found them. She went on to tell her what Elsie had said and the fact that he was in a relationship with someone else and didn't want to be taken back but just forgiven for all the bad things he had done. Lorna was amazed at what a saint he now sounded but wasn't sure she believed it.

"Did Maddie recognise him at the home" she asked her Mum.

"No, I think she has no memory of him at all so this could come a bit hard for her, especially as she is so attached to Bill now" replied Irene. "I just don't know what to do for the best, you girls deserve to know your father but I don't want to put you at risk again"

"Mum, we are older now so you don't need to protect us so much, I will promise that no harm will come to Maddie and I think that we perhaps should take up Mr Deeley's kind offer and meet him on neutral ground" she replied. "If he is as sorry as he claims then I think we will all know if that's true once we meet him. I will go and speak to Mr Deeley tomorrow and arrange something for after school and leave it to me to talk to Maddie".

"Thanks love, you are a real angel and a great comfort to me, you know that don't you" replied Irene.

"Yea, I know now go and put some dinner on Mum, I'm starving" said Lorna giving her a kiss on the cheek and then dashing upstairs to have a chat with Maddie.

It was sometime later when Irene called them both down for dinner but it had given Lorna enough time to sit Maddie down and explain everything to her. Maddie was initially worried that her Dad would replace Bill who she had grown increasingly fond of over the past few months since he had been visiting regularly following Harry being drafted, and she wasn't sure if she wanted to meet her Dad but Lorna had explained that whilst it was her decision it couldn't hurt and that they would all go together.

Maddie had a hundred and one questions for her Mum over dinner and Irene answered them as honestly as she could with Lorna interjecting when she could see her Mum getting a bit upset. The conversation ran well into the night after they had gone to bed and Maddie finally fell asleep due to pure exhaustion at the end.

The next morning she had made up her mind that she would go with Lorna and her Mum but wanted their assurance that they could leave if she felt uncomfortable. Lorna went as promised to see the Head Master who was happy that she called by and after asking her how she had been getting on since she left school agreed to let them have the use of his office and would phone Mrs Robertson at the home and arrange a time after school for the following week.

Lorna asked if she could speak to Mrs Robertson on his phone now which he was more than happy to do and after speaking to her Lorna felt a bit relieved at hearing what her Mum had told her the previous evening.

In the meantime, Arnold had been on tender-hooks for days, hoping against hope that Irene and the girls would agree to meet with him. He spoke at length to Sue about it and asking her whether he was doing the right thing and should he tell his Mum yet who he knew would be overjoyed at the prospect of seeing her grand-daughters again.

"I think that yes you should meet with them if they are

agreeable but if for any reason they say no then you will have to accept it and move on with your life. That doesn't mean you have to forget them and in time Irene and the girls may change their minds but it has to be their decision so give them all the time they need" said Sue. "And as for telling your Mum, I think it would be best if you hold fire on that score for a while you don't want to get her hopes up too much".

"You're right of course" replied Arnold. "What would I do without you, you have been a real help and support to me since I have been here and I love you for it."

"You what?" Sue said rather shocked.

"Oh gawd, I have done it now haven't I? Well the truth is Sue I think I have fallen for you in a big way, I will understand if you don't feel the same, after all my track record with women is pretty poor" he replied but he couldn't say anymore as Sue planted a big kiss full on the lips.

"Oh you daft old fool, don't you realise that I feel the same way you big chump? How could I not fall for you too, you may have had a tough time in the past, who hasn't, but that's just it, it's in the past and we must not look back but forward to the future" said Sue as she continued to have her arms wrapped round him.

"Now would you like me to check with Elsie to see if she has heard anything?" she continued.

"Yes please, I don't think my nerves will take much more anticipation" replied Arnold.

Sue then went off to Elsie's office and knocked quietly on the door before entering. Elsie was on the phone at the time so Sue turned to leave but was beckoned to sit down whilst she finished her call.

"Well that's a bit of coincidence, I was just going to come and find you and Arnold, I have just spoken to Lorna, Arnold's eldest daughter and she informs me that they are willing to meet with you both at the school one day next week. I am happy to release you both for the afternoon on whatever day you decide, just let me know. Is Arnold aware you are here?" said Elsie

So it was the girls and their Mum waited with Mrs Robertson in Mr Deeley's office the following Tuesday after school, all feeling rather apprehensive but trying not to show it when there was a knock on the door from Mr Deeley's secretary to say that Mr Pashley and Mrs Gillis had arrived and were they ready to receive them.

Lorna looked at her Mum whilst Mrs Robertson gave her a reassuring smile and patted her hand in a way to say that she was sure that it would all work out just fine.

Irene nodded and the secretary stood to one side to let them both in. Irene immediately felt the old familiar feelings of fear and unhappiness return when Arnold entered the room but they soon vanished when it dawned on her that his whole persona had changed and he seemed calmer and less uptight than he had been when they were together. She, however, was still wary and feeling protective of the girls and was looking to Lorna for the support that she would no doubt receive from her when Lorna broke the ice for her.

"Hello father, you are looking well" said Lorna rather quietly.

Maddie was holding tightly to her hand not quite sure whether to speak to him or not.

"I'm very well thank you" he replied with tears springing

to his eyes. He couldn't quite believe that he had managed to find them and it struck him very strongly how much he had thrown away all those years ago. "Thank you so much for agreeing to meet with us". He had intentionally mentioned Sue to prove that he had moved on with his life and that he had received the help he had so desperately needed and had acknowledged the fact all be it too late to make a difference to them.

He then bent down to speak to Maddie as he could see how shy she was with him.

"I must say you did some lovely singing the other day at the Retirement Centre" he said with an unknown softness to his voice which took Irene completely by surprise. "I don't suppose you remember me there do you?".

Maddie looked at Lorna very uncertain as to whether to reply but Lorna gently coaxed her forward whispering that it was okay.

"Thank you" she whispered politely and then feeling a bit more brave "Are you coming to live with us?"

Arnold laughed gently with tears streaming down his face now. "No love, but I would like to see you from time to time from now on, do you think you would like that?" he replied.

Maddie gave a shy nod and returned to Lorna's side and grabbed her hand once more.

Mrs Robertson was observing these exchanges with a small smile of encouragement to Arnold and Sue and suggested that perhaps she should take Lorna and Maddie outside so that Irene could discuss what they wanted to do in the future. Lorna was happy with this idea and felt more comfortable with Sue being present as she seemed to have a very calming effect on everyone which she guessed was an excellent tribute especially in her line of work.

After the door closed Irene couldn't help but ask why Arnold wanted to find them considering the reason she had left with the girls.

"Please believe me when I say how sorry and ashamed I am at the way in which I treated you" he replied. "I have had a lot of professional help since then as I hit rock bottom and was led to a great guy called Roger at my local Spiritualist Church who helped me no end along with some therapy sessions I attended. I am a changed man but I don't expect you to take me back, indeed the opposite as I have found a wonderful lady who has helped me become the man I am today" he said as he turned to give a loving glance to Sue who was holding his hand the whole time.

It struck Irene then that she no longer had anything to fear from him anymore and nothing could hurt her or her girls again and she also felt that it would be safe for them to rebuild a relationship with their father and she hoped in time that perhaps they could all be friends in the end.

They chatted for a few minutes more before Irene felt that perhaps it was time to head home and she promised that she would contact him to arrange a further meeting once she had spoken to the girls.

"Thank you so much Irene for coming today, I wasn't sure if you would and I would have understood if you hadn't and I am eternally grateful" said Arnold.

"You have made a huge difference to him today" said Sue. "You have no idea what this means to him, he has been looking for you for so long and he was overjoyed when he spotted Maddie at the Centre the other day. You have done a marvellous job bringing them up on your own, not an easy task I'm sure".

"Thank you Sue", said Irene. "It is a great comfort to know that you are there for him, he used to be such a loving man and I'm sure you are now experiencing that again and I wish you both a lot of happiness"

Sue approached her then and gave her a reassuring hug which was followed by Arnold which surprised Irene that she didn't instantly recoil from his contact which is what she suspected would happen. It was a good start to the rebuilding of their relationship and one which could only lead onto a brighter future.

She kindly thanked the secretary on the way out and with the girls they left the school and hurried on home to get their dinner.

They chatted on the way home and Lorna confirmed what Irene had been thinking in that perhaps it wasn't such a bad thing that Arnold had found them and now that he had built a relationship with Sue the pressure was off as to whether he would be expecting something more.

Maddie also seemed okay with the idea that she would be seeing him again and after Lorna had reassured her that he would not be taking Bill's place in their affections she was happy to go along with any arrangements that were made in the future.

It had been a very emotionally charged day and they were glad to get home to the comfort of familiar surroundings. They chatted more over dinner and then all had an early night and for once Irene slept well with all the fear that she had pushed to the back of her mind now completely dissolved and it wasn't till quite late that she awoke the next morning.

She pottered downstairs just after nine o'clock and discovered a note from Lorna to say that she hadn't want to disturb her so she had got Maddie ready for school and took her before she went off to the cafe. She hoped that she had slept well and not to worry about anything now as she was sure that it was all going to work out well.

Irene smiled to herself and again was very thankful for her eldest daughter who had been such a help and support to her and she couldn't help but feel totally relieved and happy that the future looked bright.

It was whilst she was sitting have a quiet cuppa that spring morning when there was a ring on the bell which seemed rather urgent so she quickly dashed to the door and pulled it open to find a rather tired and grubby soldier standing before her. It took a split second for her brain to register that it was Harry standing before her, almost fit to drop and he fell into her arms in a huge bear hug.

"Oh my gawd, Harry" she screamed between tears. "You've come home, Lorna is at work at the moment, oh my goodness I must go and get her".

"No, please don't" he replied "But if I could just freshen up a bit I'd like to go over there and surprise her".

"Yes, of course, you can luv" Irene said forever thankful that he had come home safe. "How long have you got" she enquired knowing only too well that it wouldn't be long.

"Only till the weekend I'm afraid, have to report back on Sunday early" he replied. "But wanted to come here first".

Irene knew that Bill was quite likely to pop round later as he often stopped to dinner mid-week but didn't want to alert him to the surprise but would find it difficult to hold her excitement until Harry got back from the cafe with Lorna.

A short while later Harry emerged back downstairs looking like a new man and whilst still in uniform it was a clean set of clothes and looked mightily handsome before he dashed out of the door eager to see his beloved.

Meanwhile Lorna was sitting having a quiet cup of tea with Bertha in the cafe, business had been a bit quiet and despite being lunchtime there was still not a lot of customers in. Lorna was sitting with her back to the door when she noticed that Bertha had fallen silent and a huge grin had appeared on her face.

"Oh my dear, look what the cat has dragged in now" Bertha joked.

Lorna turned to see what she was talking about and was rushed upon by a huge embrace. It took a moment to realise who it was and she immediately started to sob uncontrollably with the relief at seeing him again after so long with no letters or contact.

They held each other for what seemed like an age when Bertha reappeared with a huge steaming pot of tea and two massive slices of carrot cake knowing all too well it was her carrot cake they ate when they had their first meeting here in her cafe all that time ago.

They thanked Bertha but the tea went cold and the cake uneaten as they continued to hug and chat in between times, savouring every moment they had. Harry had told her how long he had and once Bertha had overheard this she insisted that Lorna take him home and enjoy the short time they had. She could manage quite alright on her own for the rest of the week.

Lorna gave Bertha a huge hug and assured her that she would make up the time and couldn't thank her enough as she practically dragged Harry out of the door hardly giving him time to thank Bertha himself.

Meanwhile, Bill had indeed popped round to Irene's and was a bit puzzled at how excited she seemed but wouldn't say why. He eventually put it down to the relief she must be feeling following her meeting with her ex.

They chatted about the meeting for a while and was pleased to hear that it had gone well and that her fears had been put to rest. Bill had become increasingly fond of Irene and was feeling very protective towards her and the girls and enjoyed spending time with them all. It somehow made him feel closer to Harry who he knew adored them all.

CHAPTER TEN

It took Lorna and Harry some time to reach home as they couldn't believe that they were together again and stopped at every park bench to sit and embrace. Lorna still had tears in her eyes and Harry would gently wipe each one that escaped away with a gentle touch.

They chatted about their plans for the future and on the way home Harry reminded Lorna that they still needed to get her engagement ring sorted out. So they decided it was a good a time as any to pop into the town and see if they could get it done.

She was surprised when he stopped outside a rather exclusive jewellers and pulled her inside.

"We can't afford to get it done here" cried Lorna knowing full well it was quite an expensive shop. She knew that as she had often passed by the window when on her errands and always admired a very pretty bracelet in the window.

"Well it just so happens that the owner is a friend of my Dad's" replied Harry. "And I'm sure he will be able to make the alterations for me a bit cheaper".

"Besides I seem to recall every time we have passed his window you look longingly at something there and I would love to know what it is".

"Oh if you must know, it's that pretty silver bracelet in the window with the double heart in the middle" replied Lorna "It so reminds me of one that my Mum had which Dad destroyed in one of his rages. I had always liked it and Mum said I could have it one day".

"It that case my darling wife-to-be you shall have it, I'm sure that I can come to some arrangement with old Bert here" said Harry with a smile.

"There's no need for that, it is so expensive" replied Lorna never wanting anything more than to have Harry by her side.

"Oh yes there is, I have some money saved whilst I have been away and I want you to have something special to show how much you mean to me" he replied.

"But I have that with the beautiful ring you gave me" protested Lorna, but Harry was having none of it and asked Bert to show it to him after sorting out the size required for the ring.

"Oh my goodness" said Lorna who was shocked how gorgeous it looked on her slim wrist but wasn't happy to accept it due to the cost. "I can't accept this, it's far too much money".

"I am sure we can do something about that" said Bert. "I'll tell you what, if you buy the bracelet I will re-size the ring for free, how does that sound?" He was happy to help them as he knew full well what a courageous man he must be to fight in a war to keep him and his family safe.

"We are forever in your debt for what you are undertaking in Europe and I am guessing that you are only here for a short while, so I think that this bracelet has just gone in our sale which starts about now" he continued as he looked at his watch with a twinkle in his eye.

Harry couldn't thank him enough and Lorna was so overjoyed she leant over the counter and gave the man a kiss on the cheek.

"Thank you so much, are you sure it's okay and that you can afford this?" said Lorna worrying that it was too much for Harry to fork out.

"No problem, at all luv and thank you kind Sir for your kind thoughts" replied Harry as he paid Bert who kindly provided him with a plush velvet box in which to keep it but also guessing that Lorna probably would never take it off her wrist.

After saying thanks again and arranging to call back in a couple of weeks to collect the ring they said a hurried goodbye and dashed from the shop eager to get home to show off her bracelet to her Mum. On the way they stopped at Maddie's school to pick her up and as the children all piled out of the school Maddie shrieked with delight when she saw Harry stood there and rushed into his arms with such a force that she almost knocked him over.

"You've come home, you've come home" she shouted covering his face with little kisses. "I've missed you so much, are you coming home with us?" she asked suddenly afraid that he wasn't staying.

"Sure am, little one, hope that's okay" he replied with a huge grin on his face.

Maddie nodded uncontrollably and insisted that he piggy-back her all the way home.

Irene and Bill were talking in the kitchen whilst she prepared dinner when Bill heard the key in the lock.

"Here's Lorna and Maddie by the sounds of it" said Bill. "I'll put the kettle on and make a cuppa".

"Don't you worry about that Bill luv" said Irene. "You go and have a sit down and I'll bring one in in a moment" knowing full well that Harry was with them which was going to be a huge emotional surprise for Bill.

Bill went out as instructed and suddenly there was a huge scream from the hallway and the penny dropped with Bill as to the real reason that Irene was so excited. She obviously knew Harry was going to walk through the door any moment.

The scream was followed by uncontrollable sobbing from all four of them in the hallway and Irene came out to usher them all into the front room and placed a full pot of tea on a little side table.

Bill was beside himself with immense relief at having his only child back with him safe and sound and didn't want to think about the short time that he was likely to be there.

Lorna was also keen to show off her new bracelet and after lots of oohing and ahhing they asked if they had set any plans for the wedding. They replied that they hadn't as it was so difficult what with Harry having such a short time home and not knowing how long this dreaded war was going to go on for. Plus they had no where they could live as they were not sure if there was anything they could afford at the moment.

It was at that point that Irene had an idea and she asked if Bill could give her a hand with the dinner in the kitchen for a moment and practically dragged him off the sofa to join her.

"I have an idea that might help them if you are agreeable" said Irene.

"Fire away luv, what did you have on your mind?" replied Bill.

"Well, what I was thinking was if it was alright with you" she continued somewhat apprehensively. "If you would like to move in here, perhaps into Lorna's room and then Harry and Lorna could live in your place and give them a good start, what do you think?"

"I must say that seems to be an excellent idea and I sure would like to have the company. I must admit I hate coming home to a cold dark empty house after work" he replied. "But are you sure that you are not worried about what the neighbours would say?" He was genuinely concerned about her reputation and whilst he had no qualms about doing as she had suggested he knew that some folk could be a bit funny about such goings on.

"Oh don't you worry about them, they know you very well now and I have been through worse times I don't really care what they think, we both deserve some happiness and if it feels right for both of us then so be it" she replied.

So that was how the decision was made, Lorna and Harry now had a home to make their own and wouldn't have the worry of the expense of furnishing it, plus they were near enough to see her Mum and sister on a regular basis. There was also the added benefit of Bill having company in the evening and for Maddie having a father figure around which pleased her no end.

There was celebrations all round that evening and soon it was time for Harry and Bill to go back home. Harry took Lorna out into the garden before he left and asked her something which came totally out of the blue and took her a bit by surprise. It had been a hell of a day what with the new bracelet and now the thought that they had a new home they could go to once they were married that she couldn't possible imagine anything more.

"I know this is a bit sudden and I don't know how you feel or if there is enough time but how about we get hitched before I go back?" said Harry.

Lorna just threw her arms around his neck which was answer enough for him.

"I don't care how soon it is I will do everything I can to arrange it although I have no idea where to start but I am sure Mum will help me" replied Lorna.

They embraced for a long time with both of them crying with joy and then went inside to tell the others of their plans and asking their advice as to what to do next.

The next couple of days were like a whirlwind of arrangements and announcements. The local vicar was all too pleased to marry them on the Friday which would give them a couple of days before Harry had to report back. Lorna, Maddie and her Mum went shopping for outfits the following day with all the clothing coupons they could lay their hands on. The neighbours on hearing the good news had all donated some of theirs so that Lorna could get something special. Lorna was overjoyed when Bertha had given her a bit extra in her wages once she heard the news and insisted that they all came back to her cafe which she would close for the day for a bit of a party afterwards.

Lorna hadn't been working for Bertha for long and was very touched at her generosity and couldn't thank her enough and was so grateful for the extra few pounds for her outfit and it would also help to get Maddie and her Mum something nice too. Bertha had also said she would bake them a nice cake....carrot of course in recognition of their beginnings!!

They all were exhausted after a full mornings shopping and Lorna was anxious to get back to Harry as she didn't want to waste any time that she had to be with him. They had all found some lovely outfits with Lorna's being a lovely cream two piece suit with a long flowing skirt and cute little hat to match. They just about managed to have enough coupons to purchase it all and Irene almost cried when she saw her.

In the meantime, Harry and his Dad had been busy too getting themselves kitted out. Bill's employers at the coal merchants were all too happy for him to have the day off and were so pleased to hear that Harry had come home safe and that they had decided to get married whilst they had the chance that they also gave him a wedding present of a year's supply of coal and were more than happy for Harry to take over the rental of the cottage.

By the end of Thursday everyone was totally exhausted from all the arrangements and when Lorna and Harry said goodnight it was with tears in their eyes at the joy of tomorrow being their wedding day which whilst it would make it more difficult for Harry to return to the barracks on Sunday it gave him the peace of mind that Lorna was finally his and was praying to a quick end to the war so he could come home and spend the rest of his life with her.

Friday dawned a beautiful spring day with daffodils and crocuses bringing a lovely splash of colour in all the gardens and parkland. The wedding was set for 11 o'clock and Lorna was up bright and early to make sure she wasn't late. Irene styled her hair beautifully with lots of tumbling curls with fresh flower intertwined. She had decided to forgo the hat as her hair looked so much better with the flowers. She looked stunning when she came downstairs fully dressed and Maddie's outfit complimented her well as she was dressed in a soft pink dress that Irene had made from some material she had stashed away.

Harry and Bill and a few neighbours were all at the church in plenty of time and one of Harry's friends from the coal merchants had agreed to be Best Man and his boss said he would take a few photos for them. Harry was somewhat nervous as he awaited for the love of his life to arrive and both Bill and his Best Man Tom assured him that she would be there and not to worry.

All of a sudden the church bells started to ring out and Maddie came slowly down the aisle enthusiastically scattering tiny coloured paper punches that Bill had acquired from the office. It made a pretty carpet of snow-like covering that scattered as the gentle breeze blew through the open church door. Lorna had wanted Bill to give her away but after a lot of thought and talking it through with her Mum it was agreed that Arnold should be the one to undertake the role which Bill whole heartedly agreed with. It had made Arnold's day to be asked as he had felt for sure that that was the one thing that he had blown every chance of doing and it touched him greatly to learn that he had been given a second chance.

It was with great pride and emotion that he led his eldest daughter down the aisle and Harry was equally choked to see such a vision of loveliness coming towards him.

The day went off without a hitch and everyone, including the vicar piled into the Bellview for a traditional knees-up afterwards. Bertha did them all proud with the spread she had laid on and the elaborate cake caused great jollity when it was revealed that it was in fact a cardboard mock-up and was lifted to reveal a small carrot cake underneath. The rationing had hit hard and whilst Bertha had extra supplies for the cafe it still wasn't enough to produce the fine cake she would have wanted too. Needless to say she had still managed to find tiny soldier and bride figures which she had perched on the top. Lorna and Harry were still very grateful for the huge effort that she had put into their special day and proudly presented her with a large bouquet of garden flowers that they had chosen together from their garden.

Later on they cleared back some of the tables and someone had brought a gramophone player in and some records and they all had a dance with everyone insisting on dancing with the beautiful bride. It was a long tiring day but an extremely happy one and they all waved Harry and Lorna off as they set off for their new home in one of the coal firms borrowed cars. It was rigged up with dozens of tin cans and streamers with a huge white ribbon bow attached to the front grill.

Once home and after Harry had swept Lorna up in his arms to carry her over the threshold they just fell into each other's arms, with the knowledge that time was so short and precious that they couldn't bear the thought of being parted again. They were amazed when they walked into the front room to find that some of Bills colleagues had been in whilst they had been at the reception to do the house up. There was balloons and ribbons everywhere and sitting on the side table was a chilled bottle of homemade wine and two delicate crystal glasses along with two heart shaped biscuits with their names neatly iced on the top.

When Harry carried Lorna upstairs they both noticed the stairs and landing had a trail of the coloured paper punches like the ones that Maddie had strewn before them in the church. This continued into the bedroom which again had been decorated with balloons and more punches covering the eiderdown.

Harry and Lorna both laughed at all they saw and really appreciated all the effort their friends and neighbours had gone to to make their day such a special one.

They were both very tired after such an eventful day but as they fell into bed Harry's passion for his new bride knew no bounds and Lorna equally was stirred with the emotion of the day. Harry was a gentle lover and was careful not to hurt Lorna and whilst Lorna was a bit apprehensive about this moment, welcomed him to her with equal passion and their final union was one of sweet delight.

They finally fell asleep in each other's arms and were awoken early the next day to sunshine streaming through the bedroom window as they had forgotten to close the drapes before falling into bed.

They both laid there for some time just listening to the birds singing and each other's heartbeats until the previous night's passion consumed them again and they gave themselves to each other once more.

It wasn't till mid-day that they finally surfaced and wandered downstairs whereupon Lorna cooked up a delightful breakfast which was consumed with vigour.

Lorna was just clearing away the dishes and putting them in the sink when Harry came up behind her and kissing her neck turned her round in his arms and thanked her so much for agreeing to marry him and that it was the best day of his life.

"I love you so much" said Lorna "I don't know what I am going to do without you when you go back tomorrow".

"Please don't think about it luv" replied Harry as he once more swept her up in his arms and carried her back upstairs.

The day was over all too quickly and Lorna was distraught at the thought of having to say goodbye to him in the morning, so much so that she clung to him all night and whilst their lovemaking was sweet and tender Lorna cried the whole time. This upset Harry as he thought he was hurting her but she reassured him that it was not the case but just that she was heartbroken to have to say goodbye tomorrow.

The emotions the following dawn were very tense and it took forever for Harry to don his uniform as they were clinging to each other constantly. Eventually the dreaded hour arrived and Lorna was sobbing so hard as he walked away from her up the garden path. She went back inside and just curled up on the sofa and cried.

This was how Irene found her daughter later that morning and insisted that she come home with her and stay with them for a while. She could sleep with Maddie in her room who had missed her terribly since she had been gone. It had helped to have Bill there who had played endless games with her to keep her occupied but she still missed her big sister and was very distraught to see Lorna in such a state.

"I'm okay Maddie luv, I am just very sad that Harry has had to go back to war" she explained to Maddie.

"Don't worry, he will come home again, I just know it" replied Maddie.

"Let's hope so" smiled Lorna as she felt more tears springing to her eyes She didn't want to cry anymore as she knew it would upset Maddie and she was being so sweet in trying to reassure her, but she just didn't know how she was going to get through the coming days and maybe weeks or months if this blessed war didn't come to an end soon.

CHAPTER ELEVEN

The following months were very difficult for all of them, they all missed Harry terribly and they heard through the grapevine that Harry's battalion had been posted deep into enemy lines and again the letters stopped coming. Lorna went to church every Sunday and prayed hard asking to keep him safe and continued to talk to the moon each night hoping against hope that Harry was talking to it too.

Bertha tried to keep her busy at the cafe but she noticed that Lorna often went very quiet almost into a dreamlike state and she knew she was deeply worried about her new husband.

Bill too was finding it difficult and the two of them often chatted till late into the night about Harry and all the plans they had when he came home. The conversations usually ended up with both of them crying on each other's shoulders but it was good to have each other there to share their grief.

The summer came and went and Lorna tried to keep busy by making the garden as pretty as a picture and with Bill and Irene's help it ended up a lovely place to sit and soak up the summer sun. Maddie often came to stay to keep

Lorna company as it was easy for Lorna to take her to school on the way to the cafe and pick her up afterwards.

Bill had taught Lorna to drive that summer and this gave her a bit more freedom and she enjoyed helping Bertha by going to pick up supplies for her for the cafe. She was now saving to buy a small car as it would be lovely to surprise Harry when he got home and had sworn his father to secrecy about it.

It was early autumn when she arrived home after dropping Maddie off after school one Friday and was busy hanging some new curtains she had made when there was a knock on the door. That's strange she thought as the family always came straight in as the door was always unlocked and they would just call out to let her know who it was.

She carefully climbed down from the small step ladder she was on to go and open the door and found a uniformed officer standing there with an envelope in his hand and a solemn look on his face. Lorna's heart immediately sank and a wave of nausea swept over her. She was petrified as to what the envelope contained as she took it from him with a trembling hand and shut the door. She had dreaded this moment and had often seen and heard of others that had received correspondence of this nature.

She sat down on the settee with tears in her eyes as she looked at the type written envelope in her hands, so afraid to open it but knowing that she must. So with trembling hands she tore it open to read that Harry Weston was reported as missing in action and that his battalion had been badly hit in a confrontation that had taken place in a war torn area of Germany. It gave no further information and Lorna just crumpled into a heap on the floor.

Some hours later Irene and Bill called round with some more material for the kitchen curtains only to find the house in darkness and the front door unlocked.

"Hello Lorna luv, are you there" called out Irene as she wandered through into the front room.

There was nothing but silence that greeted her and she saw Lorna in the dim light crumpled up on the floor by the settee with a letter tightly grasped in her hand.

She gently prised it from her fingers just as Lorna came to and burst into a further flood of tears when she saw her Mum stood before her.

"Bill, Bill, come quick!!" shouted Irene as she read the contents of the letter.

"He's gone Mum....he's gone" sobbed Lorna just as Bill came dashing into the room.

Bill stopped dead in his tracks when he saw the distraught look on both their faces and his heart immediately sank when Irene handed him the letter. He knew what it contained before he read it but opened it anyway to find his worse fears become reality.

"Now Lorna, don't you go thinking the worse, lots of soldiers disappear and turn up later. He has probably been captured and is in a camp somewhere" said Irene trying to sound more composed than she felt.

Bill in the meantime had sunk onto the settee with his head in his hands and tears sliding silently down his face. How could this happen he thought to himself, Harry was all he had left in the world and he just didn't know what he was going to do without him.

"Bill luv, come on you have to be strong too, I'm sure he'll turn up, you have to have faith" said Irene softly. She had grown to adore this heartbroken man before her and couldn't stand seeing them both in such pain.

Bill looked at Lorna who was still sobbing quietly and decided that he must be strong for her so gathering himself together he said,

"Your Mum's right luv, I'm sure he will be holed up somewhere. I think you should come back with us tonight, you can sleep in your old room and I'll sleep on the settee".

Irene then went upstairs to pack some overnight bits for her daughter and almost cried aloud at the thought of what the future may hold for them all and silently praying that Harry was safe somewhere.

Once back at Lorna's old home Irene went a made a huge pot of hot cocoa and brought it through to Bill and Lorna who were sat huddled together on the settee giving what comfort they could to each other. It broke Irene's heart to see such a scene but she knew that she had to be strong and be there for both of them.

They all decided that they would take a trip to the barracks the next day to see if they could find out anything more about Harry and what may have happened but until then they had to get some rest although none of them could possible contemplate how they would sleep but the cocoa was a good start.

Meanwhile across the Channel in the depths of war torn Germany Harry's battalion had been captured during an arduous battle, they had already lost several men and a number had been injured. Luckily Harry had remained unharmed apart from some cuts and bruises and he considered himself very fortunate. However, now was a different story as they were all loaded onto a rickety old truck and transported to god knows where.

They seemed to have been travelling for hours with no break or food and drink and Harry was beginning to wander if he was ever going to see his beloved Lorna again. He managed to work his way to the edge of the truck and peered out of the old wooden slats. It comforted him no end when he saw the moon and prayed that Lorna was looking at it too and sent her a silent message of hope. He figured by now that she probably was aware of his disappearance and was hoping that she was not thinking the worse. His Dad would also be in a state but they had each other and Irene who he had no doubt would hold them all together.

After about eighteen hours the truck shuddered to a stop and they heard the guards shouting "Raus, raus!! They all piled out with some of them stumbling badly as they had been cooped up in such a tiny space for so long it took a while for their muscles to adjust.

They found themselves in a transit camp and one by one they were interrogated. Harry knew that under the terms of the Geneva Convention he was only obliged to give his name, rank and serial number, however, the guards did try some clever questioning to obtain more information but most of his colleagues were also too clever to fall for their tricks.

They were all then piled into train carriages which had been shunted into a siding near the camp again with no food and only a dirty bucket of water to quench their thirst. The train once it was underway did stop at regular intervals this time and all the prisoners were expected to get off to relieve themselves before being pushed back on at the end of a rifle.

They travelled this way for a further few hours before it came to a halt outside a POW camp about 50km from Dresden. Harry had no idea where he was or even if he was still in Germany but no doubt he would in due course. It was daylight by this time and the sight that greeted Harry was not a pleasant one. The camp was surrounded by barbed wire with regular watch towers dotted around the perimeter with armed guards standing ready to shoot anyone that tried to escape.

Harry was led into a small draughty wooden hut which was rammed with dirty old bunk beds with extremely thin mattresses which probably housed more life than the train load of prisoners that had just arrived!

"Now what do we do" said Harry to his colleague who was stood by him looking at the sight with utter despair. He was about the same age as Harry and was missing his family terribly. His wife had just given birth to their first child when they had to leave and he talked about his little girl constantly.

"Have no idea mate" said Joe. "Will just have to make the best of it I guess, stiff upper lip and all that".

Harry laughed, it was great to have someone so positive nearby which he thought would help them all no end in getting through this. He just wished that he could somehow get word to Lorna that he was o.k. and said as much to Joe.

And so it was that they all settled themselves down to camp life which wasn't easy at times and they saw some horrible actions being taken by the guards if you didn't comply with their orders. One of the biggest difficulties they faced was the hunger, the guards would only give them two meals a day and that only consisted of a thin soup and black bread and by the end of a couple of months they all looked like skeletons wandering around the camp.

Coupled with the hunger they were all pulled out of bed at any hour of the day or night for roll-call and those that were missing were shot if they were found. Harry found this very hard to come to terms with, even more so if it was one of his own battalion but it gave him the strength to get outside no matter how weak he felt.

It was some time later that there was great excitement in the camp as the first Red Cross parcel arrived. What luxury they all thought as they unpacked such delicacies as biscuits, chocolate, vegetables and dried fruits. This gave all the men a much needed boost and some of the inmates that had been there for a number of months even received letters from home although these were heavily censored as where the ones that the prisoners were allowed to write to loved ones back home.

Harry would have loved to jot a few lines down but paper was scarce so he decided he would do whatever work he could in order to obtain some and get word back to his lovely new wife and father.

The weather was turning cold now with the onset of winter but that didn't deter the guards from pulling them all outside in the freezing temperatures for roll-call. This had a devastating effect on the inmates especially as they had not received any Red Cross parcels for weeks now and the lack of nutritious food had taken a detrimental effect on the health and minds of them all.

It was to be Christmas Eve tomorrow and it saddened Harry to think that Lorna would be spending her first Christmas as a married woman without him. He had had so many grand plans for them before he was conscripted and now they all seemed like a fairy tale so far removed from reality. He continued to talk to Lorna via the moon each night which took some explaining when Joe caught him one evening.

"You've finally lost it then mate?" he said trying to make light of what he had heard.

"It's the only thing that keeps me together whilst I'm stuck here" Harry replied. "Lorna and I made this plan to meet on the moon each night in the hope that it would keep us safe, crazy huh, but I would feel terribly guilty if I didn't do it".

"You miss her a lot don't you?" said Joe. "Know what you mean though, I'd give anything to get back to my Beth and baby Molly right now, she had only just been born when I got called up and I feel that I have missed everything". There were tears in his eyes as he mentioned his beloved family and Harry couldn't help but wonder what it must feel like to have a child and have to leave them both, it was bad enough having to leave Lorna, so much so it tore him apart sometimes.

They sat for a while then in silence each wrapped up in their own thoughts and Harry was sure as he saw Joe looking at the moon that he too was silently trying to talk to his family. He hoped that somewhere all of them could hear them in their desperate attempts to communicate and they both bent their heads and prayed hard that this would all soon be over and they would make it back to normal life.

CHAPTER TWELVE

Christmas Day dawned cold but sunny, the threat of snow had not materialised and Arnold was up bright and early with the excitement of the day. He had big plans for him and Sue today although she was totally unaware of what he had planned.

They both had been given a day off and Arnold was going to be cooking a Christmas dinner for them both at his small caretakers cottage that he had been living in since he had secured the position at the home. He had been up half the night decorating the place so it looked nice for Sue when she came over later and the smell of the small rabbit in the oven made him feel peckish already.

There was a small pile of presents under the tree in the front room some of which were for Lorna and Maddie who he had been seeing on a regular basis much to his delight. He hadn't yet taken them out on their own and although Lorna was old enough that no harm should come to them Irene was hesitant to allow him which he fully understood. His Mum had been overjoyed when he had finally told her of what had occurred and her first visit with them found her hugging them so tightly it had frightened Maddie who had no memory of her at all. It was okay now though and

Maddie was thrilled to have a granny who spoilt her no end and Arnold felt that it had helped enormously with his relationship with her.

It was just after ten o'clock when there was a knock on the door and Arnold dashed to open it complete with one of Sue's frilly pinnies on.

"Well that's very fetching" said Sue as she mocked Arnold at his appearance. "Merry Christmas Darling" she continued as she handed him a small but beautifully wrapped gift.

"Come on in, Honey" he replied and gave her a quick kiss on the lips whilst undoing the pinny and whipping it off.

"My, something smells good" said Sue as she wandered into the kitchen. "Do you need a hand with anything?".

"Nope, all under control" Arnold replied. "Why don't you make yourself comfy and I'll bring through some eggnog".

Sue wandered back into the front room just as Arnold appeared down the stairs.

"Shall we open our presents now or did you want to wait till after dinner?" enquired Arnold.

"Oh now, please. I'm nothing but a big kid at heart and haven't got the patience to wait" replied Sue.

Arnold went over to the gramophone player and put on some soft music before bending down to pick up a small box from under the tree.

"This is for you, I hope you like it" said Arnold nervously.

Sue slowly undid the wrapping paper to find a small velvet box inside and she gasped when she lifted the lid to reveal a small but perfectly beautiful gold solitaire ring nestled on a soft velvet cushion.

"I know we haven't known each other that long" said Arnold. "But you must know that you mean the world to me and I love you with all my heart. Would you do me the great honour of being my wife?"

"Oh my God" said Sue with tears in her eyes. "Yes, yes..... YES!!" she screamed and throwing herself into his arms.

Arnold breathed a sigh of relief, he finally felt that he had been given a second chance of happiness and he couldn't believe how lucky he had been in not only turning his life around but finding both Sue and his family in the space of a few short months.

They spent the rest of the day celebrating their engagement and decided to visit the home late that afternoon with some homemade fairy cakes for the residents and a tin of homemade biscuits for Elsie not only for Christmas but also to let them all know about their news.

"Oh my" said Elsie when they told her. "I expected as much would happen sooner or later, it's amazing what can happen from a dropped tray of tea cups" she laughed referring back to when they first met.

"And I have only you to thank" said Arnold "For taking the chance and giving me this job, you have not only allowed me to earn back some self-respect but you have been the reason how I found my family and love again. I can't thank you enough".

"Oh be going along with you now, you deserved the break and you have done me and the home a lot of good too you know, I don't know what we would have done if you hadn't come along when you did" she replied. "Now off you go and finish off your celebrations and I'll see you back here in a couple of days".

Sue and Arnold couldn't stop grinning for the rest of the day as they toured the home and getting to speak to everyone who were all very chuffed at the news. They finally left for home about 8 o'clock with Arnold escorting Sue home like a pure gent and with a passionate embrace they said goodbye before Arnold returned to his cottage a very happy man.

Meantime in the other Pashley home things were not quite as rosy. Both Lorna and Bill were finding it very hard to be cheerful without knowing about Harry. They had been to the barracks a number of times for news and whilst the sergeant on duty did his utmost to find out any snippet of information for them he confirmed that no news was coming out of Germany other than quite a few of the same battalion were missing in action which looking at it positively could mean that they had been captured and were in a POW camp somewhere.

Both Lorna and Bill were hanging onto this hope as if their lives depended on it and tried to remain as cheerful as possible for Maddie's sake. Irene knew how hard they were both trying and her heart went out to them. She was secretly praying that no harm had come to Harry as she knew that they would both would go to pieces should the worse happen.

Christmas came and went along with the new year of 1943, Lorna was soon to be 20 and she had been considering for some time about joining up to help the war effort in any way she could. She had learnt to drive from Bill and was used to driving about in Bertha's old van to pick up groceries for the cafe and she was thinking that perhaps she could help using that skill in some way.

She had been making some further enquiries at the local hospital when she spotted a leaflet pinned to their noticeboard about the ATS and the need for ambulance drivers. She thought that this might be what she was looking for and approached the desk to find out what to do next.

The young lady at the desk told her that there was a meeting arranged at the local church hall for later that week and if she was interested to go along and gave her some details of the time and what would be included.

When Lorna got back home after her stint at the cafe and collecting Maddie from school she broached the subject with her Mum explaining that she felt that she needed to do something to help and that as she enjoyed driving then being an ambulance driver would suit her to a tee.

"Would you like me to come with you to the meeting?" asked Irene. "Bill can look after Maddie".

"That would be great Mum" Lorna replied. "I'm sure that they will be giving out lots of information and I doubt if I will remember it all so another pair of ears would be useful".

So it was agreed that Maddie would stay with Bill and they would go over together.

They arrived at the church hall a little before it was due to start and Lorna was surprised at the number of people that were there. They found a couple of seats near the front and shortly afterwards a middle-aged lady in an ATS uniform climbed up onto the stage to introduce the evening.

After she had said her bit a variety of questions were asked which made up Lorna's mind that this is what she wanted to do. It meant that she would have to go away for a short period for some extra driver training but she expected that anyway and felt it would be all worthwhile in the long run. She would miss her family terribly but after speaking to her Mum about it she knew it was the right thing to do.

There was a desk at the back of the hall manned by another uniformed ATS member who gave Lorna a form to complete which included details of her driving experience. She said that once they have had time to review all the applications they would write to her to advise whether she had been accepted. Lorna said that whilst she was not quite 20 yet she was keen to become involved and was told that that shouldn't be a problem as the processing and training would take a couple of months in any case.

Lorna left the meeting in good spirits although she was not sure how Maddie would take the news as they were very close. She was in bed when they got home and Lorna said she would pop round earlier the next day to tell her before she went to school.

There was a fluttering of snow overnight so Lorna wrapped up extra warm and went out to scrape the vans windows just as the postman walked up the road with a letter for her. She quickly stuffed it in her pocket and would read it later once she was in the nice warmth of the cafe.

Maddie was very pleased to see her although a bit curious as to why she had come round so early.

"I have some news for you" said Lorna. "You know Mummy and I went to the church hall the other day, well it was to see if I could help the wounded soldiers by driving the ambulance".

"Wow!" replied Maddie, she was impressed that she was doing something so clever. She then realised that it would probably mean that she would have to go away and was then worried that she wouldn't see her for a long time.

"You're not going away, are you?" said Maddie suddenly very solemn and thinking that when Harry went away she hadn't seen him since and didn't want to lose her big sister in the same way.

"Only for a short while, they need to teach me how to drive very fast but safely" replied Lorna. "I don't know yet if they will accept me but I wanted to tell you as I expect if I am I will be away pretty soon".

Maddie seemed happy with this once she had got Lorna to promise to write to her as much as possible whilst she was gone which Lorna was happy to do as she would want to correspond with her Mum on a regular basis in any case.

Bertha, whilst a bit unsure about the news could understand why Lorna wanted to do this and told her not to worry about her job at the cafe and they would manage without her. After all the war couldn't go on forever and felt it would be good for Lorna to be involved to take her mind off worrying so much about Harry.

It was thinking about Harry that she remembered the letter in her pocket and pulled it out and read the unfamiliar writing on the envelope. It was not from someone she knew so quickly tore it open to find a single sheet of paper written by a Sergeant Holmes. He had been asked by Harry to contact her should he get home before him.

The letter explained that some time previously he had managed to escape when his battalion including Harry had been captured and sent to a POW camp in Germany. There were two of them that got away but unfortunately his fellow escapee had been caught and returned to the camp. Sergeant Holmes in the meantime had laid low for a number of hours in a dirty muddy ditch before finally crawling away and finding a group of resistance who helped him get back to England. He was extremely weak and malnourished and had only just arrived home with the strength to write to Lorna at an address he had memorised. It was a number of months ago he had last seen Harry but he had been well and unhurt following being interned but to Lorna it was enough to know that he was alive.

Bertha found her in the kitchen in floods of tears and when she saw the letter in her hand suspected the worse.

"Oh my dear, have you heard about Harry?" she enquired softly.

Lorna looked at her and with a big smile said "Bertha, he's alive, he's alive!"

"Oh, thank God, I have been praying so hard, is that a letter from him then?" she replied.

"No, no, it's from a fellow soldier who managed to escape and Harry had asked him if ever he got home first to let me know he was okay and he memorised my address so he could write" explained Lorna.

"It has been quite some time since the escape but I'm just glad that Harry is okay and gives me hope that he still is" she went on.

"Well, I think you must go and tell Bill the good news too" said Bertha who was almost pushing her out the door in the excitement. She was so pleased that all was well so far and insisted that Lorna take some time off so she could go home and tell the family.

To say that Bill was relieved was a great understatement but both him and Irene knew that a lot could happen in a few months so they continued to pray for his safety. It was, however, a strand of hope that they clung to together as a family and Lorna spoke at length to the moon that night wishing Harry to be kept safe at all times until he could come home.

CHAPTER THIRTEEN

Life at the camp had been made extra hard since the escape and there were severe repercussions for the remaining inmates.

All hell had broken loose when his sergeant and fellow soldier had made the escape attempt late one night and it wasn't long before they were all pulled out of bed for a roll-call as they dragged one of the soldiers back into camp and shot him dead right in front of their eyes.

Harry knew at this point that they were all in danger as the guard reloaded his gun and in broken English told them that in view of this escape attempt one other person would be shot. He was slowly patrolling up and down the rows of prisoners as he spoke and stopped in front of Harry. He forced Harry to his knees and placed the barrel of his gun against Harry's temple. Harry knew that this was it and his last thought would be of Lorna and the life she would now have to live on her own.

Whilst Harry braced himself for what was inevitably to come the guard pulled the trigger.

However, nothing happened, the gun had jammed. Harry's guardian angel was obviously there protecting him. The guard moved the gun away from Harry's head and fired again randomly into the crowd of prisoners. This time it went off and hit a fellow prisoner in his right thigh who fell down with a cry. Immediately the guys on either side of him helped him back up knowing all too well if he wasn't standing then it would draw attention to the guard and probably shoot him anyway.

There was suddenly a shout to the guard from their hut and he dashed off with no further shootings happening and Harry prayed silently thanking whoever was protecting him for saving his life. He immediately went to the aid of the injured soldier and helped carry him back to his bunk.

There was no medicines or pain killers that Harry could administer so he did what he only knew he could do and that was to lay his healing hands on the poor guy's leg to give him some relief.

The other soldiers were amazed at this as Harry had not told anyone of his gift but the immediate results were evident in that the soldier felt the pain completely dissolve away. Harry was a hero and they asked no end of questions about his ability and were keen to know if he practiced this before he was signed up.

Harry went on to explain his story and Joe who was aware of all the facts said that he should write it all down as he was sure that others would be interested to read it once the war was over.

There were no further escape attempts and Harry hoped that Sergeant Holmes had made it safely back home. He knew it wouldn't have been easy but knew that if he was successful then Lorna would be told that he was okay.

Life continued on with them all trying to make the best possible life in a bad situation and it was towards the end

Lorna's War

of the summer that Harry heard of talk of a further escape plan. Harry didn't want to be involved as the previous winters shootings were still very vivid in his mind which caused some horrendous nightmares whereupon he would wake up in a cold sweat due to the realism of them.

However, it was planned to such expert precision that Harry began to think that it would be possible although he ideally just wanted to bide his time and wait it out till the end of the war. But as Joe explained that if the Germans lost then they would probably shoot them all anyway.

This made up Harry's mind and became involved in the planning which was destined to be by way of the latrines. Not a pleasant thought by any means but the safest as the guards never went near them due to the disgusting smell and mess that they were in.

The plan was to dig a tunnel down from one of the latrines and out under the wire to a nearby wood. The original organisers of the plan had been watching the guards routine very carefully and were fully aware that each Saturday evening they had a truck load of 'ladies' brought into the camp for the guards pleasure. There would be much drinking and singing and the soldier's attention would not be on them for the whole night. There was however, the chance of a impromptu roll-call during the evening but this seemed to have fallen by the wayside over the last couple of months and they had been left alone till the following day.

Harry's immediate concern was for his fellow in-mates safety who were not escaping for one reason or another as he knew only too well what would happen to them once the plan was discovered. However, that had all been taken care of by way of faked deaths in order to get the numbers down.

Those that supposedly died had been kept in secret under the floors of the huts and fed on a regular basis from the rations of the others. Once the escapees had left the camp they would re-emerge to ensure that the numbers were the same and hence not raise any suspicions.

Everything was going to plan and of the five initial inmates that were going to make the break they all had to take it in turns in going down the latrine to help dig the tunnel. When it came to Harry's turn the stench made him physically vomit and he ended up fashioning himself a basic mask which he stuffed with dandelion heads to mask the smell.

It was late autumn 1943 when they finally broke through in the wood and it was with great celebration back in the camp that they organised the order in which they would disappear. It was agreed that only two at a time would be safe over a period of days and they all drew lots as to who would be first.

As luck would have it Harry and Joe were the first names out of the hat and they spent the next couple of days getting together some minimal belongings and collecting hastily written letters from the others that should their attempt succeed could they get them to their loved ones.

After months of organising and agonising over whether it was the right thing to do both Harry and Joe spent their final night talking to the moon and praying to be kept safe in their attempt.

As soon as the women had arrived to the guards quarters and they heard the raucous singing Joe and Harry stole out with only the light of the moon to guide them and over to the end latrine. The stench was breath taking due to being in full and still quite warm sun all day but they knew that they had to bear it if it meant regaining their freedom.

They crept without a sound and dropped down amongst the accumulated human waste and crawled as quickly as they could through the tunnel and away from the camp.

They seemed to be crawling forever in total silence as they didn't want to take the chance of being heard through the soil to a passing guard and it wasn't till some time later that the tunnel started a gentle incline to the surface.

Once they reached the exit Joe cautiously peered out and back at the camp which was in darkness with the exception of the search lights which periodically scanned the perimeter fence. Their clothes were by this stage covered in excrement and mud so they peeled them off under cover of a nearby hedge and donned some spare clothes that they had brought with them in an old potato sack.

It was at this stage they realised that they really had no idea which way to head and so they decided to head directly away from the camp as fast and silently as they could.

After a while they came to a road and using what little local knowledge they had gleaned over the years as to the location of the camp they went west in the hope of finding a small barn to shelter for the rest of the night. Suddenly there was a commotion up ahead and they both dived into the ditch just as a rambling old truck drove back past them. They heard French voices and figuring they must be near the French border and with all the bravery they could muster crawled out of the ditch and approached the direction of the voices.

It turned out that the voices belonged to members of the resistance who after satisfying themselves that Harry and

Joe weren't Germans took them both to a hide-out where they equipped them with new clothes and papers. After explaining their story it was agreed that they would arrange passage on the next transport to get them out of Germany. It wasn't going to be easy but if they were happy to bide their time they would find a safe route for them.

Harry and Joe couldn't have thanked them more and offered their help in the interim in any way possible. It was with this in mind that they were introduced to the head of the resistance team who wanted to know more details of the camp where they had come from as they had heard there was one in the vicinity but had been unable to find it safely. They were anxious to help the other inmates that were coming out and would also provide them with papers and shelter when the time came.

It was sometime later that Harry and Joe finally fell asleep after their incredibly tiring trip but they were awoken suddenly with the sound of gun fire coming from outside. One of the resistance immediately came into the room to explain what had happened and to keep quiet and lie low. Apparently a group of SAS guards had come across a couple of their members and when they had tried to run they were shot at and whilst injured they thought it safe to "play dead" until the guards left.

The injured men were brought back to their hide-out whereupon a member of the resistance who was a doctor removed the bullets but unfortunately it was too late for one of them who had lost too much blood to survive.

The other, however, whilst bleeding severely had managed to have his blood flow stemmed and Harry approached to see if he could help and laid his hands on the man's wound and with quiet concentration applied healing. The others watched in amazement as the bleeding stopped and the man came too exclaiming that all the pain had gone.

And so it was that Harry found himself not on the next transport home but staying with the resistance to help their cause by healing the wounded amongst them and any unfortunate injured prisoners they came across.

Meanwhile, Lorna had completed her ambulance training with flying colours and following a short stay back home had been seconded to the squad bound for Portsmouth to help ferry injured servicemen who had been shipped back home to various hospitals in the area.

She was enjoying her work immensely and had even been taught basic mechanics to keep the ambulance on the road. She missed her family greatly but wrote regularly and had on occasions managed to telephone due to Irene and Bill having installed one now that there was extra income coming in. All was well at home although they missed her too but with Bill there to look after her Mum and Maddie she knew they were all in good hands.

After one particular busy shift in late autumn Lorna was feeling particularly tired, she had seen some horrendous sights that day from a ship load of soldiers that had arrived and unfortunately they had lost a few on the sailing which always upset Lorna as they were so close to home and their loved ones again. She had tried to help the medics wherever she could and was often seen covered in blood and close to tears at the awful injuries that these brave men endured.

It was on one of these occasions that a young man was brought to her ambulance screaming deliriously in pain from his leg which had been amputated on board following stepping on a mine in his attempt to reach the boat.

"Harry, Harry where are you, please take this pain away" he screamed before falling unconscious on the stretcher.

Lorna couldn't help but overhear his lament and instantly rushed to his side knowing that this could possibly be her Harry of which he spoke especially as it would seem that he had the ability to heal.

After finding out his name was Joe she gently stroked his fevered brow and willing him to come to so she could speak to him.

"Joe luv, can you hear me?" she asked gently.

Joe's eyes fluttered open and looked at Lorna. "Please help me" he cried.

"Ssh" she replied. "You are safe now, we will get you to hospital and take care of the pain for you, just try and relax".

Lorna was anxious to know about the Harry of which he spoke but felt that she had to get him to hospital first and get him comfortable. She would pop along and see him after her shift had ended.

It wasn't till earlier the following day that Lorna had the opportunity of visiting as another boat load of soldiers had arrived and it was all a bit manic. Lorna was shattered having not slept for 48 hours but nothing would deter her from visiting Joe.

She found him sitting up eating some breakfast when she arrived and whilst looking a bit battered and bruised seemed to be in good spirits.

"Hello Joe" she said tentatively. "You're looking a lot better".

"I'm sorry but do I know you?" he replied thinking he would surely remember such a pretty face.

"No, you don't but I am secretly hoping that you know someone I do" said Lorna.

"Now who might that be then?" Joe said.

"Well, when you arrived I was one of the people that helped get you here and you were pretty delirious with pain and you were calling out for Harry to take the pain away" said Lorna hoping against hope that it was her Harry.

"Yes, he is a remarkable chap, got this gift he has with his hands, could help with the worse wounds I've ever seen" replied Joe. "Oh my God you're not Lorna are you?"

"Oh....thank you so much, you don't know what that means to me to know he is alive?" she cried excitedly. "Is he okay and did he come back with you?"

"Sorry, luv, no" replied Joe as he saw Lorna's face fall. "No, he's all right but he didn't come back with me, good job too as he might not have made it there were so many land mines on the beach where we picked the boat up that we lost so many".

"No, he stayed behind to carry on helping but he did promise that he would try and catch the next transport out" Joe continued. "It was hell out there and if it hadn't been for the resistance we probably would be dead now".

Joe went on to explain to Lorna their time in the camp with their escape through the latrines which made Lorna feel physically sick but wanted to know everything that her poor Harry had gone through. She almost cried when Joe told her about Harry being picked for slaughter by the camp guard and knew that Harry's guardian angel was looking after him that day.

"Harry spoke about you all the time" said Joe. "He even had me talking to the moon with him, I thought him a bit loony at first but when I tried it I found it somewhat comforting to know that my Beth and Molly were perhaps looking at the same moon too".

"Did you want me to try and contact them for you?" asked Lorna smiling knowing that Harry had been doing just as she had all those miles away.

"Oh, would you please, I'm sure she is thinking the worse and I can't wait to see them both again" pleaded Joe.

Joe gave Lorna their telephone number and Lorna promised not only to call them but would offer to drive them down to see him if he was still in hospital on her next leave.

Lorna was floating on cloud nine when she left the hospital and was soon on the phone to her Mum.

"Mum, it's me, have just had the best news ever" said Lorna excitedly down the phone. "It's Harry, he's alive".

"How do you know, luv" replied Irene hoping that what she said was true, she would hate to see Lorna get her hopes up and only for them to be dashed.

Lorna went on to tell her Mum what had happened and how she came across Joe and it was Irene's excited voice that brought Bill to the phone and she had to repeat it all again. She heard Bill sobbing on the end of the line with relief and she promised him that as soon as she heard anything else she would let them know.

Then, as Lorna had promised she picked up the phone again and dialled the strange number.

"Hello, 2465" said a softly spoken voice.

"Hello, my name is Lorna Weston, you don't know me but I am an ambulance driver for the ATS here in

Portsmouth and I have some wonderful news for you and your baby girl" said Lorna.

There was a cry at the other end. "We have your husband Joe here at the hospital, he is severely wounded but alive and he wanted me to call you. He misses you both so very much" said Lorna.

There was sobbing coming from the other end now and between tears Beth said "Oh my God, thank you so much I have been praying for him so much and we feared the worse when we heard he was missing, I felt we had lost everything".

"Well, he is o.k and been asking for you" Lorna replied. "He has helped me too as he brought news of my husband so I know exactly what you are feeling right now". "Look I have some leave due to me shortly and if Joe is still in hospital would you like me to fetch you and bring you down to see him?"

"Oh would you, that would be very kind of you" said Beth through her tears.

"Tell you what, why don't you give me your address and I'll pop by as soon as I can as sometimes leave is granted at the drop of a hat and I may not have time to call you" replied Lorna.

"You are an angel Lorna and I don't know how to thank you" said Beth.

"None needed, am so pleased to help as I know only full well how agonising your wait has been" replied Lorna.

As it turned out Beth and Molly didn't live far from a hospital in London that Lorna had recently transported a patient to. So a couple of weeks later Lorna found herself on a strange doorstep ringing the bell. Beth was overjoyed to see her and gave her an enormous hug as if they had been friends for years. Lorna immediately took a liking to this small delicate young woman and fell in love with Molly as soon as she laid eyes on her with her beautiful head of curly blond hair and infectious giggle.

They were soon on their way back to the hospital where they had kept Joe in due to an infection he had developed on his stump. It was nothing serious but Lorna warned Beth that it wasn't a pretty sight and he still had to come to terms with losing the bottom half of his leg. Beth said it didn't matter one bit and the important thing was that he was alive and been returned to them. She suddenly felt for Lorna who still didn't know the whereabouts of Harry and whether he was still o.k and she apologised to her for being so insensitive.

Beth, Molly and Joe's reunion was so sweet that it brought tears to Lorna's eyes and she made an excuse to leave them alone. She couldn't help but wish it was Harry lying there and continued to hope that he would get out alive and come back to her soon.

CHAPTER FOURTEEN

So it was that Joe, Beth, Molly and Lorna became firm friends. Joe was discharged from both the hospital and the army shortly after and she took them all home whereupon they insisted she stay overnight after the long drive.

Joe and Beth couldn't thank Lorna enough for all she had done and promised that they would be there for her if she needed anything…anything at all. Beth hugged her tight the following morning with tears in her eyes and said she would pray for her and Harry to be back together soon. Lorna was quite sad to leave them but wanted to spend some time at home with her own family before she had to report back next week.

The time flew by and soon she was on her way back to Portsmouth after a tearful farewell with Maddie who wanted her to stay. She was growing up fast and would be 11 in a few months and Lorna felt she had missed a lot of sister time with her. She said as much to her Mum who reassured her that she would be fine and they would all be together soon once this wretched war was over.

Lorna arrived back at her station with a heavy heart, she had seen so much death and destruction that it tore at her very soul to realise how many lives had been ruined by all this fighting. She was, however, determined to see it through and threw herself back into her duties with every fibre of her being.

It was going to be Christmas next week and unfortunately she was having to work through the holidays which had upset everyone badly but both Irene and Bill understood that the poor soldiers needed her right now and they could celebrate at a later date.

Lorna had just settled down in her bunk in the barracks that night when a call went out that all drivers were to report to their vehicles and get ready to depart for the docks as two boat loads of injured soldiers had arrived were being unloaded. Lorna quickly got dressed again and dashed out to her ambulance where the medics were already waiting.

They all tried to be cheerful and ribbing Lorna as to how long it took her to get there but they all knew that they were not going to be faced with a pretty sight.

"What have we got coming in?" asked Lorna as they sped along.

"Not sure" said one of the medics. "But we understand that its a number of very war torn soldiers so brace yourself, I don't think its going to be pretty".

Lorna had seen a lot in her time with the ATS but nothing could have prepared her for what came off of the boats. Apparently not only was there a number of lost limbs from the land mines but the Germans had been laying in wait for them and had opened fire on the whole group. Many had died crawling to the waiting boats and those comrades who tried to help them suffered some severe injuries in doing so. The scene was absolute carnage as the medics tried to prioritise and deal with the worse cases first.

Lorna didn't have time to think and went into automatic pilot getting as many into her ambulance as possible. Some were so badly disfigured that she couldn't even make out how old they were, she just did the best job possible and tried to save as many as she could.

Lorna was back and forth between the docks and the hospitals for hours and finally there seemed to be a lull and she fell onto her bunk and into an immediate deep sleep.

In what seemed like only minutes later she was being shaken roughly awake by a fellow driver.

"Lorna…..Lorna…..wake up, the C.O wants to speak to you".

Lorna came too and was still in a daze thinking she was in trouble for leaving her post and falling asleep.

"Oh no, I didn't mean to fall asleep but I was so tired, do you think I'm in trouble?" she asked.

"I don't know, they just asked me to fetch you as quick as I could" replied her friend.

Lorna quickly dashed over to the CO's office and knocked politely on the door.

"Come, in" said the gruff voice of the CO. "Sit down please".

"Have I done something wrong Sir?" she asked. "I didn't mean to fall asleep but I was so tired".

The CO's face softened, "No, you've done nothing wrong Lorna dear, in fact you are a model service woman, I wish we had more like you around" he replied.

"It's just that I have some news for you that may be a bit upsetting" he continued.

Lorna's heart sank, she knew that it must be about Harry and tears sprang to her eyes.

"It's Harry isn't it?" she choked.

"Yes, I'm afraid it is. He was brought in on the second boat, he is alive but only just, he came under severe sniper fire on the beach and was shot amongst other places in the back and the bullet caught his spinal cord" he continued.

Lorna was silent with tears running down her cheeks as he continued. "He is in the operating theatre now but we can't promise anything, he may be paralysed from the waist down".

"When can I see him?" sobbed Lorna not really caring about his paralysis but just wanting him to survive.

"As soon as he is in recovery, which should be in an hour or two, they are trying to repair the damage but it won't be a pretty sight so prepare yourself" he said. "You can have some time off to sit with him as long as you would like and let me know if there is anything I can do for you" he continued compassionately.

"Thank you Sir, I very much appreciate you telling me all this and for the time off" she replied as she got up and hurried out of his office.

She had to tell Bill what she had learnt so with tears in her eyes she tried to dial the number.

"Hello, Bill here" said Bill in his usual friendly manner but all he heard on the other end was huge ranking sobs and he couldn't make out what Lorna was trying to say.

Eventually after much cajoling to calm down and breathe Bill was told of what had occurred. Irene saw the colour drain from his face and immediately knew it was Lorna and feared the worse.

"Let me speak to her" Irene said with such determination, she knew she had to be strong again for them both. "Lorna luv, it's Mum here, Bill tells me that Harry has come back and in a bad way".

"Yes Mum, they are operating on him right now but they can't say what the outcome is going to be" said Lorna trying her hardest not to dissolve into another flood of tears.

"Well, all we can do is pray that he will pull through, do you want Bill and I to come down?"

Lorna wanted that more than anything but she knew how expensive and difficult it would be for them and besides they had Maddie to think about. So she told them that it was okay and she will ring them once Harry came out of recovery and let them know what the position was and please don't say anything to Maddie yet until they knew for sure what was happening.

Lorna had never prayed so hard in all her life, not even when she was trying to shut out her Mum's cries from the beatings she was getting when she was younger. She knew that she had to be there for Harry no matter what happened but she was so frightened as to what she might find.

It seemed like hours later that the doctor came and found her in the waiting room to say that they had done what they could for Harry and only time and his will to live could tell now. Lorna knew that he would want to live but she was not sure how he would react to his injuries.

"Can I go in and see him now?" Lorna enquired.

"Yes you can, he is still unconscious and pretty beaten up but I think he will pull through" the doctor replied.

That was music to Lorna's ears that he was going to make it and gave the doctor a huge hug and thank you for what he had done.

She then rushed into Harry's room and the sight that greeted her was not good, he seemed to have been bandaged from head to toe with only his right hand and face visible amongst the whiteness of the bandages.

She pulled up a chair and gently took his hand in her own and kissed it softly. There was no movement or sound and Lorna sat there for an eternity before she finally laid her head on the bed and fell asleep.

Lorna woke to the sun streaming through the window and her hand being squeezed gently. Harry moaned softly as he opened his eyes and painfully turned his head in Lorna's direction. Lorna was watching him with tears in her eyes wondering if he knew where he was. Suddenly the smile that she had missed for so long appeared as Harry realised where he was and finally home. Lorna just wanted to hug him tight but refrained from doing so due to his injuries so just gave his hand a squeeze and a loving kiss full on the lips. It was going to be a long road to recovery but one they would do together no matter how long it took.

"Well you have finally decided to wake up then you lazy git" came a familiar voice from behind her. Lorna spun round to find Joe, being pushed in a wheelchair by Beth and Molly towards them.

Lorna dashed to give them all a hug and ask what they were doing there and was told that they had received word that Harry had made it back albeit in a terrible state and that they knew they had to come down for Lorna's sake if nothing else after all she had done for them. Beth cried all the more when she saw Harry, although she had never met him she had heard so much about him from Lorna that it felt like she did and hugged Lorna harder still. They were great friends now and nothing would have kept her from coming down to support her.

They all approached Harry's bedside and Harry noticed Joe in the wheelchair and he looked devastated to see his friend who had gone through so much with him in such a way. Joe picked up on the look and said "Oh, don't worry about this, I'm being fitted for a falsie after Christmas so won't be long before I'm up and about again".

Harry marvelled at Joe's spirit and began to wonder at what state he was in looking at all the bandages he saw.

Lorna looked at Joe who returned her solemn gaze and nodded to say that it would be okay to tell him. He was a strong guy and with his own healing ability stood a better chance than most of conquering his injuries.

"O.k, give me the worse" said Harry quietly.

Lorna relayed what the doctor had told her yesterday as they all listened in dismay but Harry was having none of it, he knew that the spirit can heal almost anything and was going to give it his best shot. As soon as he was permitted he was going to be out of this bed and chasing Lorna around just like he used to do. They all laughed at the vision he produced for them and they knew that that would probably be what would happen.

"You better get your running shoes on then Lorna cos if I know this guy there will be nothing stopping him once he's set his mind on it" said Joe.

The doctor appeared then and asked them to leave and wait outside whilst he could examine Harry. He said Lorna could stay as he was sure she could help.

Once they were gone the doctor carefully removed the bandages from Harry's head and arms, both were pretty badly scarred but the doctor said they would heal. His major concern was for his back and carefully undid the bandages on his legs. Harry didn't move and his legs remained immobile the whole time. The doctor took a pen out of his top pocket and ran the top down each of Harry's feet but there was no reaction. Harry couldn't feel a thing. Lorna's heart sank, she knew this wasn't a good sign and Harry looked crestfallen and didn't know what to say.

"Now don't get disheartened, the operation went very well and these things take time" said the doctor reassuringly. "We won't know much more till we can get you out of bed but that won't be for a while yet as we need the back to stay immobile for the time being to give it the best chance".

"Lorna, can you pop to the supply room and fetch me some more dressings, I'd like to change this one" continued the doctor.

Lorna left and was immediately greeted by Beth and Joe who wanted to know the outcome. After telling them the news and getting some reassuring hugs she fetched the dressings and returned to Harry's side. Beth and Joe seemed shocked that Harry might not be able to fight this but they knew that miracles can occur in fact two already had by bringing them both back home to their families. They said as much to Lorna when she reappeared some time later and she thanked them for their support and sorry she couldn't spend some time with them but her place was by Harry's side right now.

Joe popped back into the ward to say goodbye to Harry and whilst he was gone Lorna sat down with Beth and dissolved into tears on Beth's shoulder, she knew that she couldn't appear upset in front of Harry but Beth was such a support to her that she had to finally convey her fears for the future to her as she knew that bottling it up would do her no good in the long run.

"Look Lorna luv, you have to deal with this in a positive frame of mind" she said. "You know Harry is a strong guy and with his healing ability he is bound to recover from this but it will take time. And if he cannot regain the use of his legs then it is something that I know you both can handle. Remember that what doesn't kill us makes us stronger. Joe and I are always here for you so don't feel you are ever alone.....okay?"

Lorna looked at her new friend with such gratitude that it brought tears to Beth's eyes and they hugged each other tightly as Joe returned. Beth gave him a look as if to say that Lorna was taking this hard.

"I say" said Joe trying to sound cheerful. "It's Christmastime, how about we all spend a couple of days down here with you, I have an old Aunt who lives not far from here who I haven't seen in years and she would love to meet Beth and Molly and we can be around for you and Harry if needs be".

"Oh that would be lovely, you sure it's not too much trouble?" replied Lorna. "You are such good friends but I wouldn't want to put you out".

"No trouble at all" said Beth who gave Joe a wink as if to say thank you as she didn't really want to leave Lorna in this way. "It will be nice to meet the old lady and we can make sure that you look after yourself".

"That's fixed then" said Joe as he gathered Molly up into his arms and wheeled her up to give Lorna a goodbye kiss. "We'll see you tomorrow and don't forget try and get some rest, Harry will be fine, he's a right fighter you know".

So it was that Lorna spent the Christmas of 1943 at Harry's bedside willing and praying for him to recover the use of his legs. After about a week the doctor encouraged Harry to get out of bed for the first time. It took an extraordinary amount of effort on Harry's part but he was determined to do it. They managed to get him into a wheelchair and Lorna wheeled him to the physio unit for them to work on stimulating his muscles but Harry felt nothing during the process which disheartened him somewhat.

He asked the doctor if there was any possibility that his spinal cord had been permanently damaged and was told that whilst this was possible the operation they performed would be giving him the best possible chance of recovery. He explained that his body had been severely traumatised from his injuries and he must allow time for everything to heal properly and not to try and rush things.

Lorna knew this would be difficult for Harry as he had always been such an active person and to be confined to a wheelchair was extremely frustrating for him.

She confided in Beth one afternoon that she feared that Harry would try and do too much too soon and ruin his chance of recovery. Beth said that she would get Joe to have a word with him in the hope that he would realise that he needed to slow down and it was worrying Lorna that he was trying to do too much too soon.

1944 dawned to a dreary cold and snowy climate, Lorna had returned to work but on shorter shifts in order that she could visit Harry. He had been doing well but still had no feeling in his legs and was becoming a bit down by it all. Lorna did the best that she could to keep his spirits up and suggested that he try and give himself healing. His back had healed up nicely as had all his other minor injuries so he couldn't understand why he still had no feeling in his legs. He decided that perhaps he had nothing to lose and therefore one evening whilst Lorna was working he asked that the curtains be drawn round his bed so he could have some privacy and quietly relaxed into a meditative state. It felt strange at first to perform this on himself and as he gently moved his hands slowly first down one leg and then the other he could almost feel the heat from his hands. He knew it would take a while but he was determined to persevere as it was the only hope he had left to walk again.

He carried on this healing twice a day, he didn't let onto Lorna because if it didn't work then he didn't want to disappoint her. After about three weeks he still had not recovered any feeling and was about to give up and thought he would give it one last try. This time as he ran his hands slowly down his left leg he suddenly felt a mild tingling as if the blood started to flow through his veins again. He tried his right leg to experience the same feeling and was overjoyed and given a new lease of hope that all was going to be alright.

He couldn't wait to tell Lorna when she visited later but he didn't need to say anything as the huge beaming grin he had on his face when she approached his bedside later that day was enough to tell her that something wonderful had happened.

CHAPTER FIFTEEN

By the time the warm spring weather arrived Harry had managed to get himself in and out of bed on his own and day by day he was recovering more and more sensations in his legs. He thought it was time that he tried to stand up and with Lorna by his side he lifted himself into a sitting position on the edge of his bed and Lorna manoeuvred his legs over the side.

With a huge intake of breath Harry heaved himself up, wobbled and fell straight onto the cold hard hospital floor. Lorna dropped to his side to help him up but he was too heavy for her so she shouted for help.

"Whatever is the matter?" shouted a nurse as she came hurrying up. "What are you doing down there Harry, you know you shouldn't be up".

Harry had tears in his eyes at the failure to stand, he was so sure that he would be able to do it, he found it incredibly frustrating that he had failed in such a simple thing.

"Don't worry Darling" said Lorna reassuringly. "This is the first time in months that your legs have had to take your weight, it's bound to take some time to get used to it".

Harry knew this to be true but he couldn't help but feel that he should be running around by now, this was taking longer than he had thought.

When the doctor came on the rounds later that day he examined Harry and was very pleased to see that there was some reaction when he did the foot test again. He advised that the healing he was giving himself whilst not recognised medically was indeed doing the job and he was happy that Harry should continue with this form of treatment and eventually if all went well he would be up and around in no time.

The war was still raging on in Europe and England had received some horrendous bombings especially in London and Birmingham which was too close to home for comfort. Lorna was getting more and more concerned about her and Harry's family and tried to speak to them on the telephone every week to check that they were all okay. It was on one of these calls that her Mum was sounding particularly excited.

"What are you so chipper about?" enquired Lorna gladly. "Have you got something nice to tell me?"

"Well I wanted to wait till I see you but I can't keep it to myself anymore" she replied. "Bill has asked me to marry him......and I've said yes!!"

"Oh Mum, that's the best news I have heard in ages, when is the wedding?" said Lorna, so happy that her Mum would have someone by her side, especially with her and Harry so far away.

"I was going to check with you first as you must be there so we were going to wait till Harry was well enough to come home so we could make it a huge celebration" said Irene excitedly.

"Harry is doing very well and my C.O has said he would release me from my duties once he has been classed fit to travel" replied Lorna. "I don't think it will be that long so you'd better start planning".

"Okay luv, that sounds marvellous, did you want to have a quick word with Maddie? She is so anxious to talk to you".

After a quick chat with Maddie who was so excited about the prospect of being a bridesmaid again, Lorna was called back to work for another run down to the docks for the next load of injured soldiers. Again it wasn't a pretty sight but Lorna was so used to it by now that she was almost on automatic pilot as she dealt with what injuries she could and then sped them all back to the hospital into the hands of the waiting doctors and surgeons.

She couldn't wait to get back to Harry's bedside and tell him the good news as she knew that he worried as much about his Dad being alone as Lorna did with her Mum.

Meanwhile back at the Retirement Centre, Arnold and Sue were still in the throes of organising their own wedding but money had been tight and they both wanted to save a bit more so they could have a day to remember.

The weather was getting warmer and Arnold was busy in the garden of the home when Elsie called him in to say that there had been an official looking envelope delivered for him.

He carefully removed his boots at the door and walked in stocking feet to her office whereupon he was presented with an envelope embossed in the top left hand corner with Stockman and Harding Solicitors based in Birmingham.

He had no idea what it could possibly be about as he tore the envelope open and unfolded the expensive parchment like letter.

"Dear Mr Pashley" it read.

We are currently dealing with the estate of the deceased Miss Agnes Matilda Pashley and we are led to believe that you are the only surviving relative who would therefore be due to inherit her estate.

Please can you therefore telephone this office to arrange a mutually convenient date and time that you can attend a meeting at these offices in order that we may confirm the relationship and ultimately the payment of proceeds to you should it prove that you are eligible.

Many thanks for your assistance in this matter and we look forward to hearing from you shortly.

Yours sincerely

Mr R S Stockman.

"Oh my goodness" remarked Arnold.

"Whatever is the matter?" enquired Elsie.

"It's from a solicitors in Birmingham and apparently I am the only living relative of a Miss Agnes Matilda Pashley. They want me to go to their offices to check me out and pay me the proceeds of her estate" replied Arnold.

"Who is she then?" asked Elsie.

"I don't really know, my Dad had an elderly aunt somewhere but have no idea where or even her name, I never met her to my memory" replied Arnold.

"I think you had better give them a ring, you can use my office phone if you like" said Elsie as she left him to it to give him some privacy.

After speaking to them for a short while Arnold emerged

from Elsie's office and asked if he could have some time off the following Wednesday to travel to Birmingham for the meeting. Elsie was more than happy to help, Arnold thanked her and said he would be back as quickly as possible.

"Take your time, luv" said Elsie. "And I hope it is good news for you, you never know you might even be able to bring that wedding forward" she said with a smile.

Arnold couldn't wait to tell Sue the news but they were both very busy rushing around for the rest of the day that an opportunity didn't arise. When Sue finally found out she was very excited for Arnold but he told her not to get her hopes up as it could all turn out to be nothing.

And so it was Arnold climbed aboard a packed train the following Wednesday with directions in his pocket as to how to find the offices feeling a little apprehensive about what could transpire but at the same time feeling excited as to a possible brighter future for him and Sue.

He found the offices with ease and was immediately taken by how elaborate they were. He walked across a plush carpet to the reception desk to let them know he had arrived and was offered a cup of tea whilst he waited.

Shortly after, a short stocky man approached him and introduced himself as Mr Harding and to follow him to the office where Mr Stockman was seated behind a large, ornate oak desk. He immediately arose and shook Arnold's hand and asked him to take a seat.

After going through a few preliminaries whereby Arnold had to give some details of his father along with past know addresses and dates of birth and death it was clear that Arnold was indeed the only surviving blood relative of Agnes and that her entire estate was bequeathed to him.

"How much are we actually talking about here?" asked Arnold.

"Well following the sale of her properties and personal effects and deducting any costs we estimate the final sum to be in the region of £3,000" replied Mr Stockman.

Arnold was shocked, he had never thought for a moment that it would be that much and it took a while for it to sink in.

"Are you okay?" asked Mr Harding.

"Oh, I'm sorry, yes fine, I just didn't realise it would be that much, I've never had that sort of money before" replied Arnold.

"Well, if we can be of any assistance to you in managing anything then please let us know" said Mr Stockman kindly.

"Thank you" said Arnold "But I have some idea where some of it will go, you see I have been saving up to get married and I thought it would never happen but now we can go ahead with our plans".

"Well, can we here at Stockman & Harding Solicitors be the first to congratulate you on your forthcoming event and may we wish you and your dear lady a long and happy marriage" said Mr Stockman with a smile. "Now if you would like to give me your details I will arrange for an account to be opened with us whereupon you may draw your funds at any time that suits you".

After giving the necessary information to them and receiving the confirming paperwork detailing the breakdown and costs of the inheritance along with their assurances that the money will be invested to obtain the maximum return, Arnold left their offices with a real spring in his step. He couldn't wait to get back to tell Sue and was so engrossed in planning what he wanted to do with the money that he suddenly realised that the train had stopped at his stop and he had better get off before it pulled away again.

He arrived back at the home late in the afternoon and immediately went to Elsie's office to let her know what had happened as she had been so good to let him have time off for the trip.

"Well, how did you get on?" enquired Elsie pleased to see that he looked extremely pleased with himself.

"Marvellously, thank you" he replied as he went on to tell her what had transpired.

"I would like to make a donation to the home" Arnold continued. "You have been so good to me by giving me a chance with my previous track record and it is so appreciated. I would like to pay for the roof of the Garden Room to be replaced as we both know how bad it needs doing" he said with a grin.

"Oh my, I can't let you do that, it would cost too much and it's your money. I don't expect you to be responsible for such an expense" said Elsie completely shocked that he would offer such a kind gesture.

"I insist, you came to my aid when I needed it most and now I would like to return the favour" he replied.

Elsie was so struck by his act of generosity and finally agreed to accept his offer as it would seem that Arnold would have it no other way. She knew when she hired him all that time ago that she saw some good in him and time and time again over the years she had been proved right.

Arnold left her office that day on cloud nine and immediately sought out Sue who was preparing the residents tea. She was over the moon when Arnold told her the good news and they started to make some definite plans for their wedding which thanks to Agnes would now be coming about a lot sooner than they originally thought it could.

There was one other debt that Arnold wanted to repay to the best of his ability and so on the next day off he had he took a trip to see Irene. He had heard that Lorna had joined the ATS and her husband had been shipped back recently severely injured so he wanted to do something to help by way of repaying all the heartache and aggravation he had given them in the past. He knew he couldn't turn back time and eliminate all he had done but he was hoping that by helping them out financially would go in some way to heal the past.

It was with this intention in mind that he knocked on the door of 7 Spilsdon Avenue a couple of weeks later. Irene opened the door and was shocked to find Arnold there. She still did not entirely trust him which was understandable considering all she had endured with him but to give him his due he did seem like a changed man.

"I'm sorry to call unannounced" he said. "But there is something quite important I would like to discuss with you".

Bill was out getting some groceries and said he would be back soon as she was a bit apprehensive about letting him in when she was there on her own but he reassured her that he would do her no harm and it wouldn't take long.

Irene conceded and showed him through to the kitchen where she was tackling the week's laundry and he sat down at the kitchen table with his hat in his hands not quite sure where to start.

He explained about how he had received the letter from the solicitors and about the old Aunt that had died who he never even knew but he was the only heir to her estate. Irene congratulated him on his good fortune but not sure where it was all leading.

"I know I was a complete rat to you when we were together" he said. "And I realise now how afraid you must have been and your reasons for fleeing with the girls. I also know I can't change what has happened but I would like to give you some of my inheritance as a way of saying how sorry I am that you had to go through all that. There was never any doubt that I was a complete mess and was not man enough to realise what I was doing wrong but now I do and would like to give you and the girls £1000 to do with what you wish."

Irene just stared at him in silence, wanting to pinch herself to make sure that what she had just heard was real.

"I appreciate what you have said and your reasons for feeling obligated to give us some money but I really can't accept it, it wouldn't be right".

"I insist" said Arnold. "You have put up with so much from me and you and the girls must have struggled for so long that I feel responsible to make some sort of amends. I know money can't wipe out the past but hopefully it can make a better future for you, that is all I have to say" he continued as he placed a fat brown envelope on the table and got up to leave.

He let himself out of the door as Irene came running out behind him shouting

"Thank you so much and I forgive you and hope you now have a good life".

Arnold walked away from the house a different man, it wasn't just the fact that he had helped them out financially to give them a better life which they deserved, it was knowing that Irene had forgiven him which meant the world to him and he felt that he could now get on with his life in peace without the terrible conscious he had been harbouring all these years. His step was a lot lighter and it was like a great weight had been lifted from his shoulders. He knew he had done the right thing.

CHAPTER SIXTEEN

Bill found Irene still amid the washing when he got home with the shopping and she was sitting at the kitchen table with a large envelope in her hands, just staring into space.

"What's up luv?" said Bill not sure what could possibly have happened in the short while he had been out to do the shopping.

"You will never believe what has just happened here whilst you were gone" said Irene. "I've just had a visit from Arnold and he has come into a substantial inheritance from an old aunt he never knew and he was so sorry about how he had treated me and the girls in the past he wanted to make some sort of amends and give us some of it. He appreciated it couldn't wipe away what had happened but he genuinely was sorry for what had occurred and wanted to help make my life better".

She then handed Bill the envelope which he opened with a gasp.

"There must be hundreds of pounds in here" he exclaimed.

"One thousand, to be precise" replied Irene. "I told him I couldn't accept it but he insisted so what could I do?"

"A THOUSAND POUNDS!" screeched Bill, "You know what this means don't you, it means that we can buy a small place of our own, get married earlier than we thought and still have some left to help out Lorna and Harry".

"That's just what I was thinking" replied Irene. "Do you think there will be enough to buy Lorna and Harry a small place of their own too?"

"I should think so" replied Bill. "Now you pack that washing away and we will do it another time, or even hire someone to do it for us" joked Bill. We will then pick up Maddie from school and go out for a slap-up meal to celebrate".

So that is how they found themselves at the best restaurant in town and tucking into the best food they had had in ages. Maddie thought the whole thing amazing as she had never eaten out at a restaurant before and felt she could easily get used to the idea!!

Meanwhile and totally unaware of her Mum's good fortune, Lorna was having a rest from work there had been a quiet spell and whilst the war was still raging the news was good and it looked like England could be victorious. The casualties being shipped back were far fewer than the previous months and Lorna found she had time to spare to visit Harry who was making a great recovery. Whilst he wasn't ready to run any marathons he was managing to get himself about quite easily with the aid of some sticks. He was still very frustrated on how slowly the healing process was going despite such a serious injury to his spine but Lorna was just happy he was alive and safe back with her again.

It was early summer when Lorna was spending a warm Saturday with Harry out in the hospital gardens when she received a tap on the shoulder and when she turned round found her Mum, Maddie & Bill stood there. Lorna shrieked with delight wondering why they were there and how they had managed the fare for this surprise trip.

Maddie was ecstatic to see Lorna & Harry again and insisted on plonking herself on Harry's lap despite warnings from Irene to be careful.

"What's brought this surprise all about then?" asked Harry to his Dad knowing full well how much it would have cost to get them all down here.

"We have some excellent news" replied Bill "But I'll let Irene tell you as it was her idea that we surprise you".

Irene went on to tell them of the surprise visitor and at first Lorna was a bit suspicious as to his motives but on hearing the rest of the tale was overjoyed at their good fortune.

"Bill, said he would like to come down and see how you were doing" said Irene "So I replied why don't we, we could make a weekend of it and see the sights if you were up to it Harry".

Bill ideally wanted to speak to Harry's doctor to see if he could be discharged and brought back home and upon discussing it further they decided to all go and talk to him together.

They all trotted back into the hospital in search of him and found him in his office having a quick sandwich. They apologised for interrupting his lunch and would come back later but he insisted that they stay and asked what he could do for them.

After explaining what had happened and what they hoped they could do the doctor looked through Harry's notes and said that in view of his substantial recovery and the facilities that the hospital had near them, he was quite happy for him to be discharged and to report on a weekly basis to their local hospital for assessment.

They were all overjoyed at the prospect of returning home but they still had to go and see Lorna's C.O for her to be released from duty. This they duly did and it was agreed that she could leave the regiment at the end of the month which would give them time to find a replacement driver.

"Well, that's sorted then" said Irene. "How about we all go out to dinner to celebrate as we have something else we would like to discuss with you both".

Lorna and Harry couldn't possibly think what else it could be as so much had happened but looking at Maddie who seemed fit to burst they knew it would be good but she had been sworn to secrecy.

So it was later that day when they were all seated in a cosy little fish restaurant that Irene and Bill relayed that they had been looking for little houses as they had planned to buy their own place from the money and that they had found a large cottage that had recently been converted into two small ones which they thought would be ideal for them both.

"We would like to buy both of them, Bill, Maddie and I would live in one and you and Harry could live in the other" explained Irene. "That is if you don't mind living next door to your parents" she said to both of them.

"But Mum, that's your money, we can't expect you to buy us a home of our own too" replied Lorna.

"I know dear, but it's what both of us would like and it would help you two out especially if Harry has to stay off work for a while till he recovers" said Irene.

"That's very generous of you Irene" said Harry. "And I must say it would be a weight off my mind as I was somewhat worried about how we would survive financially if I am laid up for much longer".

"Well that's settled then" replied Bill. "As soon as we get back I will make the arrangements, I know you will love the place, it's very pretty and plenty of room for any additional family members" he said with a wink in Harry's direction. Lorna caught it and blushed, they had been talking quite a bit about starting a family but felt that the time wasn't right and had decided to wait.

The end of the month soon rolled around and there was tears all round at the barracks where Lorna had spent all her time. They all wished her well and to keep in touch and presented her with a huge bouquet of flowers and a pretty silver necklace to remember them by. Lorna was sad to go as she had built up some good friendships with the other drivers as they all understood how traumatic their experiences had been. She promised to write and keep them updated with Harry's progress and welcomed them all to visit if they were ever passing by their way.

Harry was duly discharged from the hospitals care and again the nurses were sad to see him go but understood that it would be in his best interests to go home. So clutching the paperwork which he needed to present to his local hospital he hobbled out of the hospital with Lorna by his side to a waiting ambulance that was going to take them to the train station.

However, much to their surprise, the driver of the ambulance that had become a close friend of Lorna's sped past the train station and when Lorna exclaimed that she had missed it was told that she had been given permission to take them all the way home on the proviso that she report back with the new address details so they could visit if they were in the area. Lorna and Harry were more than happy with this and were so glad that they didn't have to cart all their luggage on and off a train.

The drive home was a pleasant one with lots of chatter and song singing to pass the time and it wasn't long before they were pulling up outside 7 Spilsdon Avenue, possibly for the last time.

"Thanks for bringing us home Alma" said Lorna. "Would you like to come in for a cuppa?"

"Ooh wouldn't say no, am absolutely parched" Alma replied. So they all piled out of the ambulance and let themselves in. Irene was overjoyed to see them so early as they thought their train wasn't getting in till later that day. After some introductions to Alma they all sat down to tea and cakes that Irene had spent all morning baking with Maddie's help.

Maddie was getting very excited about something and she whispered in her Mum's ear and Irene said yes she could tell them if she wanted.

"We have got a surprise for you" she chirped. "But we can't tell you, we have to show you. Can we go now Mum please, can we, can we?"

"Only if Lorna and Harry are rested enough, did you want to come too Alma?" replied Irene.

"Yes please, I love surprises, that's if you don't mind Lorna?" she said.

"Not at all, where are we going Maddie?" Lorna said with a smile.

Lorna's War

"Not telling, you just have to follow us, it's not far I promise" said Maddie feeling all grown up at keeping the secret till the last minute.

The sun was still shining when they left and as they walked through the park Maddie was getting more and more excited. They finally walked down a pretty little lane and Maddie stopped in front of a beautiful pair of cottages and turned to grin at Lorna and Harry.

"This is yours and our new home, may I present No.1 & 2 Wisteria Cottages" Maddie said proudly.

Lorna, Harry and Alma gasped in delight.

"My goodness they are beautiful" said Alma. "Is this going to be your new home?"

"Is it?" asked Lorna to Maddie

Maddie gave her a huge grin and handed her a key. "It already is" she said. "We have been getting it ready for you for when you got here so you could move straight in" she was giggling now and Lorna had a sneaky suspicion that there were more surprises inside.

They weren't disappointed either, when Lorna and Harry walked through the pretty wisteria covered entrance they were met with the most delightful front room, quaint ornate stairway and through to the most relaxing kitchen Lorna had ever seen. There seem to be flowers everywhere and glimpsing through the pretty kitchen window it seemed that the garden was full of them too.

"Come upstairs, come upstairs" insisted Maddie as she was pulling on her sisters skirt.

They all followed her upstairs to the front bedroom and found the bed strewn with lovely pink rose petals. The whole room had a lovely warm cosy feel to it as they were then dragged through the rest of upstairs to see the tiny bathroom decorated with beautiful rose wallpaper and then onto a second bedroom where Maddie proudly advised everyone was to be her niece or nephew's nursery. They all laughed when they were shown a little cupboard over the stairs which they were informed was to be their toy cupboard.

Everything had been decorated for their homecoming and neither Lorna nor Harry could fault their choices, it was all done exceptionally well and they both could see how much hard work they had put into it in such a short space of time.

"Does that mean we can stay here from now?" asked Lorna.

"Sure does" said Bill. "Ours isn't quite ready yet as we wanted to make sure yours was ready to move into for when you got here".

Lorna threw her arms round Bill's neck and gave him the most ferocious hug as Irene stood by and watched with tears in her eyes.

"Thank you both so much, you don't know how much this means to us and to have you so close by too is an added bonus" said Lorna with tears streaming down her own face. "How long till your place is ready?"

"Oh should be finished in the next couple of weeks or so, just have to finish painting the bathroom and putting down some lino in the kitchen and we should be done" replied Bill.

"Oh goody" squealed Maddie. She had missed her sister so much and couldn't wait to be living next door to her.

There suddenly was a knock on the door so they all went downstairs to find Bertha standing on the doorstep with a basket of groceries.

"Thought you might like some grub to put in them there cupboards!" she said grinning and hugging Lorna at the same time. She was so pleased to see her back home and that Harry had safely survived his ordeal. They all wandered back through to the kitchen where Irene had put a kettle on to boil.

"Who's for tea then?" she called out to a rapturous shout from everyone.

"Surely that's my job now Mother" said Lorna with a smile and immediately settling into the role of housewife.

"Oh, o.k, I'll have two sugars in mine then" Irene replied.

They all spent the rest of the day sunning themselves with tea and cake in the pretty back garden until Alma said that she should get back and Irene, Maddie and Bill escorted her back to her ambulance. Bertha joined them and left Lorna and Harry to enjoy the peaceful surroundings of their own first home with no worries how they were going to find next month's rent.

They both laid on the freshly mown grass and looked up at the sky and saw the faint glow of the moon which brought back all the memories of when they were apart and would talk to the moon each night so they would feel closer to each other.

They knew then and there that they were going to be very happy here and they talked quietly on all that had happened over the last few years, the heartache and terrible scenes they had witnessed in this dreadful war and the good times when Harry had come back and the joy that that had brought.

It seemed like a start of a new era for them, one that was to be filled with immense joy and laughter and they both couldn't wait to get it started.

CHAPTER SEVENTEEN

Lorna and Harry spent the rest of the summer enjoying their new home and helping Bill finish off next door so they could move in as soon as possible. Many a happy evening was spent after they moved in in chatting to the early hours of the morning before retiring to their respective homes. Lorna and Irene couldn't have been happier. Maddie hankered after sleeping in Lorna's spare room once a week on the pretence she needed to get used to it for when she stayed to look after her new niece or nephew. This always brought a smile to Lorna and Harry's faces as they were trying to grant her wish as soon as possible. They weren't worried though as they knew these things took time and they both had been through a lot, they just hoped it would happen soon.

It was about two months after they had moved in that Harry was being woken each night with terrible nightmares, it was coming to a stage that he didn't want to go to sleep at night which wasn't helping his recovery which up to then had been progressing well.

Lorna had confided in her Mum as to how worried she was and Irene had suggested that perhaps he should speak to

Frank at the Spiritualist Church to see if there was anything he could suggest to help.

Lorna later suggested this to Harry who also thought it might help so later that day they both went down to the church in search of Frank to see what advice or help he could give.

"What sort of dreams are you having?" enquired Frank.

Harry went on to explain that they started off normal enough but then he was taken back to the battlefields whereby he was frog marched to a cave by the Germans and tortured to give confidential information with regard to the movements of his regiment. He then wakes up at the moment they shoot at him.

"Well it seems to me that you are suffering from some sort of post traumatic feelings which is understandable considering what you have gone through" said Frank. "We have been having some success with other injured soldiers with hypnosis to clear the emotional blockage this has caused if you would like to give it a try".

"I'll give anything a go if you think it will help" replied Harry.

"I can't guarantee the outcome, but it can't hurt to try" said Frank.

Over the next few weeks Harry visited Frank on a regular basis and found that by releasing the pent up unconscious emotions through hypnosis seem to lessen the severity of the nightmares and subsequently they stopped altogether. However, in its place Harry kept getting the name Isla Oakfield coming to him in his dreams which he couldn't understand as he knew of no-one by that name. He thought he would mention it to Lorna but it meant nothing to her either although she did recall that her mother's maiden name was Oakfield so perhaps she ought to mention it to her.

So the following morning Lorna popped next door to see her hoping that she could throw some light on this mysterious name.

"Hello luv, wasn't expecting you today" said Irene as she stood at the kitchen sink washing up.

"Hi Mum, just popped by to give you an update on Harry" she replied. "It seems that the hypnosis has cured the terrible nightmares but something quite odd has replaced it".

"Oh I am so glad that it has worked, bless him, he has been through so much and seeing such terrible things can cause all sorts of repercussions" she said. "What's this odd thing then?"

"Well I am hoping you can help actually. Harry keeps having this young voice coming to him saying her name is Isla Oakfield and that she is o.k." Lorna voice trailed off as she heard her Mum drop the plate she was washing and went strangely quiet.

"Are you o.k. Mum, does that name mean something to you?" said Lorna immediately concerned that this had shocked her Mum so much.

"Oh my goodness, I must sit down" said Irene, visibly shaken by what she had said.

"What is it Mum, please tell me" said Lorna now worried that it was something bad.

"Isla Oakfield was my sister, she died when I was young, she was only seven years old and we lost her to scarlet fever. I used to pray so hard that she was o.k now but never managed to get any messages from her, that's why I joined the Spiritualist Church in the hope that she might come through but she never has. Did Harry say anything else?" enquired Irene.

"No that was about it, why have you never mentioned her to me before?" asked Lorna.

"Well your Dad never believed in the after-life and forbade me to speak to you about it and he was so cross about me going to the church that I was afraid to go against him in the fear of another beating. Then when we finally fled I tried going back but still nothing ever came through so despite wanting to still believe that she was o.k I was beginning to lose hope that I would ever get a message so I tried to put it all behind me" said Irene quite tearful now.

"Perhaps we can all go to the church together and see if Frank can use hypnosis on Harry to get any further messages. I will have a chat with him later" said Lorna as she gave her Mum a reassuring hug. "I'm sure Isla is fine and is watching over you all the time".

"Thanks luv, I'm sure you're right but it would be lovely to know for sure" Irene replied wiping the tears away on her apron. "You run along now and let me know what Harry says later".

Lorna went back home and found Harry asleep on the settee and when he woke about half an hour later Lorna told him what she had found out about Isla.

"I dreamt of a little girl just now, thought it might be some sort of premonition that we were going to have a baby girl" said Harry. "Perhaps we better get your Mum in here and I can describe her to see if it was Isla."

Lorna immediately popped next door to fetch her Mum and Harry described the pretty young girl in his dream.

"She had beautiful long golden hair and was dressed in a powder blue dress with lace on the bottom edge and smart shiny shoes" said Harry.

Irene suddenly burst into tears at this point as it was an exact description of Isla and she was wearing the dress that she was buried in as it was her favourite.

"She mentioned she was with a Hilda and that she was all better now and not to worry. She then skipped away to an older lady who picked her up and carried her away, that's when I woke up" said Harry.

"Oh Harry, luv, you have no idea what this means to me" sobbed Irene. "Hilda was our Mum who was so heartbroken at losing Isla that she never fully recovered from the loss and it wasn't that long after that I lost her too. I was married to Arnold by then and he could never understand what I was going through and forbade me ever to speak of either of them so I just had to bottle it up and get on with my life".

"Well you don't have to do that anymore" said Lorna. "You talk about them as much as you want, I'm sure that is why she came through to Harry to finally give you the peace you so desperately needed".

Harry took Irene's hand and told her that if any other messages came through she would be the first to know and to take some comfort in that they both were alive and well on the other side and she would see them both again one day.

"But not too soon I hope" joked Lorna which made her Mum laugh and they spent the rest of the afternoon chatting about families and those they had all lost.

Lorna and Harry chatted late into the night that night as it seemed that the hypnosis had unlocked a further gift in addition to his healing that was still working wonders for him to such an extent that he could get about quite well now without the support of sticks. He still had trouble with walking any great distance as it made his back ache something terrible but after what he had endured that was the least of his worries.

It was a couple of nights later just before Maddie's 11th birthday that Harry shook Lorna awake in the middle of the night saying that Isla had come back and was warning him of an accident that was going to take place. It involved something falling but he couldn't make out what it was but had an inkling that his Dad was involved. This worried Harry as his Dad was still undertaking some strenuous work at the coal merchants, which he shouldn't have been doing but they had been so short staffed since most of the workforce had been conscripted into the forces that those that were left were taking up the slack.

Bill wasn't so sure he believed this when Harry told him the next day but promised to be careful and did take some heed to the warning as he had witnessed Harry's healing ability so who was to say that he couldn't receive messages now as well.

Harry was on tender hooks all the next day and breathed a sigh of relief when he saw his Dad walking down the path later that afternoon. He dashed out to see if he was o.k. And his Dad just gave him a big bear hug and said "Thanks Son, I think you saved my life today".

When Harry asked why he was told that his Dad was due to help unload a truck full of loose coal with a colleague but at the last minute was called into the office to take a phone call.

"The funny thing was that there was no-one on the other end when I picked up the phone and when I went back outside there was a great commotion as the load had avalanched out of the back of the truck and would have buried me alive had I been there. It was several tons of the stuff so I would have probably been crushed" said Bill still somewhat shaken by the whole episode.

"Well we must thank Isla for tipping us off Dad, now do you believe me?" replied Harry.

"Without a doubt mate and I want you to tell me of every other message you get o.k?" said Bill.

Lorna was amazed when Harry relayed the story to her and said perhaps he should go along and help at the church as it was possible that he could develop this further and perhaps help other people.

So it was that Harry found himself back at the church and sought out Frank again to tell him what had transpired. Frank listened with great interest at what had developed since he had helped Harry with the nightmares and whilst he was glad that he had not had a recurrence he was even more pleased that this had led to a greater spiritual level.

"Each of us have our own spirituality which is a private journey on your own personal path" he explained to Harry. "We are taught certain philosophies as children but we still need to find our own way. Our inner guidance will lead us to be drawn in the right way and in your case Harry it would seem that this would be the area of medium ship, especially as you have already discovered the gift of healing. I truly feel that this awakening you have experienced is meant for you and by understanding and applying this gift it will enhance your own spirituality and hence take you on the right path for your private journey".

"Yes, but what do I do now" replied Harry. "I have only had a couple of messages and that was for the family, how do I channel messages for people I don't know?"

Frank went on to explain that it was not something that could be forced but he already had the channels open he just had to trust in the gift that he had and when faced with someone who needed a message then it would come through as clear as the conversation they were having now.

Harry thanked Frank for his time and promised to attend the next meeting they had at the church whereby Frank would introduce him and not to worry it would be made clear that this was his first time and not to expect too much although Harry may be surprised.

Both Lorna and Irene were keen to hear what had happened on his return and encouraged him to go along and just see what happened.

Harry had no further visions or heard no other voices until that meeting and it was shortly before he was due to set off for the church then he kept hearing 'Stan' and the number 42. He couldn't make any sense of it and mentioned it to Frank when he arrived.

"It could be a message for someone that is coming along tonight" explained Frank. "Just try and sit quietly and focus on it and some more details may come to light".

Harry did just that and as the congregation filed in and took their seats he heard 'fourth row from the back'. Harry scanned the audience and saw a middle-aged woman sitting there next to an older woman who he guessed was possibly her mother.

The evening started with Frank introducing two other well established mediums who instantly linked up with various people in the audience and when they had finished Harry couldn't help but notice the woman he had been drawn to early looking somewhat crestfallen at not having received a message.

"We now have a young man who has not been advertised as coming on stage this evening" announced Frank. "But as he is new to this please do not expect too much. He spoke to me earlier this week as he had been receiving a message that he could not apply and I therefore suggested he come along tonight to see if it was acceptable to any of you".

Harry climbed up on the stage with an unexpected feeling of confidence that this was what he had meant to do and had no fears that the original message he had received would be leading to a whole lot more.

"I have a strong feeling that the message I have is for that lady in the fourth row from the back" he said pointing directly at the woman he had identified earlier. "There is a man here that has given me the name Stan and a number 42, does that mean anything to you madam?"

"Oh my goodness" she exclaimed with tears in her eyes. "That is my husband and he was on his 42nd mission when he was shot down. I only heard this morning that he had been killed in action that is why I'm here".

"He is saying that he is fine and it was a very quick and painless passing" continued Harry. "Who is Daisy?"

"That's our daughter, she will be eleven next week and was the apple of her Dad's eye" replied the woman.

"Well Stan is singing Happy Birthday to her and has asked for you to tell her that he will always be looking out for her and indeed for you both" replied Harry.

"He is also saying not to worry about money and to look in the bureau in your front room, especially in the middle cubby hole" continued Harry.

"Yes, I will do that" replied the woman.

"Please can you let me know how you get on" said Harry. "I'm somewhat curious now!" he said with a smile.

The woman nodded and whilst tears were streaming down her face she looked more at peace than what she did when she came in earlier.

Harry left the stage to a great applause and he felt elated and happy that he had helped someone that was in so much need. He knew that he had finally found his vocation and that with Frank's help there would be numerous other people who he could give reassurance and peace to and he looked forward to it no end.

CHAPTER EIGHTEEN

All their lives drifted on in relative peace despite the war still on although there was murmurings that it was shortly going to come to an end. The Germans seemed to be retreating and whilst a number of areas of England had been severely bombed especially London, the great British spirit were not going to let that get them down and rebuilding had begun in earnest.

1945 dawned with still no peace on the horizon and life continued to be fraught for those with sons and husbands away from home. However, it was on a hot morning in May that they finally heard the news that they had all been hoping for, for so long. The war was finally over and Britain was victorious. There were street parties everywhere and everyone was in very high spirits. Harry had fortunately been declared too injured to return to his regiment but he was still overjoyed to hear the news and hoped that all his captured colleagues would now make a safe return.

He was now a regular at the church and demand was growing for private sittings with him. More often than not it was with young women with young children who sought him out for news of their loved ones and it broke his heart when a message came through from them as he knew it would change their lives forever. They all tried to reassure him that what he told them was a comfort to them but he still found it very hard to deal with and would often arrive home feeling very down at the hard messages he had to relay.

The middle aged lady who he had had his first reading with had stayed in touch as promised and was pleased to inform him that she had indeed checked her bureau at home and found some insurance papers which advised that a substantial sum of money was due to her in the event of Stan's death. She went on to say that this had helped her tremendously and was able to buy her own house which of course lessened her financial pressures. She had been so grateful to Harry for this insight that she wished to make a donation to the church so Harry put her onto Frank who dealt with such matters and who was equally amazed as to the outcome and encouraged Harry to continue in this valuable work.

It also turned out that her daughter Daisy was Maddie's best friend at school and Maddie was beside herself with admiration for her brother-in-law at what had transpired, it was a small world indeed.

They often had Maddie, Daisy and her Mum Trish over for tea on a Sunday and would have great heart to hearts whilst the girls played in the garden.

It was on one of these visits that Harry suddenly had the urge to ask Lorna about a baby boy that was being helped through by Hilda, her grandmother.

"I'm sorry luv, I can't relate to that at all" she replied.

"Well, he is insisting that he belongs to you" said Harry.

"That's odd then, but perhaps I had better check with Mum" said Lorna somewhat confused.

Lorna's War

"You know Harry is always right, so there must be something in this" said Trish eager to find out who this little lad was.

So the following day Lorna checked with Irene but to no avail, Irene couldn't place him either and told Lorna that something would surely come to light soon to solve the mystery.

They didn't have to wait long as it turned out as it was some days later that Lorna was beginning to feel very poorly and put it down to something she had eaten. However, the nausea remained and she awoke each morning very light headed and on a couple of occasions had fainted as she got out of bed this was also accompanied with severe stomach cramps.

Harry was getting very concerned and none more so when he received a shout from the bathroom one morning to find Lorna in tears on the floor in a pool of blood.

He quickly phoned for an ambulance and they whisked both of them off to hospital. In the meantime Irene had seen the ambulance arrive and had dashed outside in her dressing gown worried about her daughter. She just had time to see her being carried out on a stretcher and Harry quickly told her what had happened and would give her a ring once they were at the hospital and had found out what the problem was.

Irene was beside herself with worry and it took Bill some time to calm her down and tell her that Lorna was in the best hands but if she wanted he would drive them both over to the hospital as soon as they were dressed.

The journey to the hospital was quick and it wasn't long before Lorna was being wheeled into the emergency theatre. Harry paced nervously outside wringing his hands in worry.

It was about an hour later that the doctor approached him to say that he was sorry but Lorna had lost the baby.

"What baby? He exclaimed. "I didn't even know she was expecting."

"Well, it was very early on in the pregnancy so it may well have been that Lorna was not aware or sure herself" replied the doctor.

"But she wasn't sick in the morning or anything" said Harry, quite shocked at the news.

"Not all women experience morning sickness and she may have just thought her period was late for a number of reasons and perhaps didn't want to get your hopes up before she knew for definite" explained the doctor.

"Is she going to be alright and will she be able to have children after this?" enquired Harry who was more worried now not only for Lorna's health but for the emotional burden it would put on her if she was now going to be childless.

"There's absolutely no reason why she cannot go on to have a healthy pregnancy in the future but may I suggest that you give it at least a couple of months before you start to try for a baby in order to give her time to heal properly" replied the doctor.

At that moment Irene, Bill and Maddie came dashing through the door and with tears in her eyes Irene rushed up and clung to Harry wanting to know what had happened. After he explained and reassured them that Lorna was going to be fine he left them in the waiting area to go in and see Lorna who by now had been made comfortable in the recovery ward.

Lorna burst into tears when she saw Harry approach.

"I'm so sorry" she cried. "I didn't know".

"That's alright Darling, the doctor has explained everything to me and he says there is no lasting damage and there is no reason why we cannot go on to have another baby" reassured Harry.

"Were they able to tell whether it was a boy or a girl?" asked Lorna.

"They were not sure but they think it could have been a boy" replied Harry.

The penny then dropped for both of them. Harry's vision the other day when her grandmother had brought a little boy through with a connection to Lorna must have been him. It must have been then that the little chap passed over. This, whilst a traumatic time for both of them brought them great comfort to know that he was safe and looked after on the other side by her maternal grandmother and happy in the knowledge that he would always be around them thanks to Harry's gift.

Irene was also overwhelmed to know of the connection and hugged Lorna tightly when she went into see her and whispered that everything was going to be okay and she would see her little boy again one day but in the meantime he will always be with her.

Lorna was released from hospital later that week on the understanding that she should take things careful and not to do any heavy lifting. Bertha was happy for her to have a few days off and popped round on the odd occasion with tasty treats from the cafe to spoil her favourite "employee".

Maddie called round every day to do little chores for Lorna and Lorna loved the time they spent together chatting in the garden afterwards. Maddie was becoming a lovely young lady despite only turning twelve in a couple of months and Lorna valued her help no end. They often had heart to heart discussions about most things and when Maddie came crying to her a few days later Lorna was extremely concerned.

It turned out that Maddie was hitting puberty and had started her menstrual cycle of which she knew nothing about and was extremely frightened thinking that she was going to die. Lorna took her to one side and explained everything and gave her the necessary equipment to cope with this huge event in her life along with the promise that she would talk to their Mum, something which Maddie had been scared to do.

The two sisters were now closer than ever and they both knew that they could confide in their utmost secrets with each other. It was because of this about a month later that Lorna told Maddie that they were trying for another baby but not to tell anyone until they knew for definite. Whilst Maddie was overjoyed she was also very anxious about a further miscarriage and insisted that she called round every day to do the heavy chores. Lorna laughed at her eagerness and said she would be careful but she couldn't be wrapped up in cotton wool but she would be extra careful.

It was mid-August that Lorna & Harry took a trip to the doctors for the result of the test and to their joy it was confirmed that she was expecting and the baby was due at the end of March the following year. Lorna made Harry promise not to spill the beans as she wanted to tell Maddie on her birthday first which was only in a couple of days. Harry reluctantly agreed although he didn't know how he was to contain his excitement but he knew how close Lorna had become with her sister so he didn't want to spoil her 'birthday surprise'.

The 17th of August dawned hot and sunny and Maddie dashed around to see her sister quite early. She was still more than happy to do the chores despite it being her birthday but she was also excited to see what they had got her for her birthday as they normally tried to spoil her when they could.

Lorna and Harry were both up and dressed when she arrived much to her surprise but they knew it wouldn't be long before she appeared.

"Good morning birthday girl" they chorused together and proceeded to sing Happy Birthday to her.

Maddie gave them both a huge hug and plonked herself down on the settee amongst the presents that were waiting there for her. After a lot of 'oohing, aahing and thank you's Maddie gave them another massive hug. She really appreciated everything they got for her but suddenly she was worried as they both had a strange look on their faces.

"Is something wrong?" she asked getting concerned.

"No, not at all, it's just that we have another present for you but you can't have it just yet" they said both grinning by now.

Maddie looked confused so Lorna whispered in her ear that come the end of March next year she will have a little niece or nephew to look after.

Maddie shrieked with delight and said that was the best birthday present ever and hugged them both again. She then proceeded to instruct Lorna to take things very easy and not to do any chores as she would come round every day after school to do them.

"And what about your school work young lady" asked Harry. "It is important that you don't let that slip otherwise we will be in all sorts of trouble with your Mum".

"Oh, that reminds me, I must go and tell her as I'm guessing she doesn't know" she replied as she ran out of the door in a grand hurry to relay the news.

Lorna and Harry followed her as they knew that her Mum would only dash round, dressed or not to congratulate them. They both arrived as Maddie was relaying the news and both her Mum and Harry's Dad started to cry with happiness. Maddie took control of the situation and told them all to sit down as she was going to make them all a cup of tea and a celebration breakfast.

They all spent the rest of that morning celebrating the good news and making plans for the future, it was still early on in the pregnancy but Harry had the comforting feeling that this time it was all going to go well but he was going to make doubly sure by taking extra care of his darling wife as she was the most precious person in his life.

CHAPTER NINETEEN

The months just flew by and whilst Lorna was very anxious during the first few months of her pregnancy she gradually became more relaxed as time went on and was ecstatic when she felt the baby kick for the very first time.

It was now January 1946 and Harry had been doing well giving a number of readings each week to the general public and had been making quite a name for himself. Irene and Bill had married shortly after Lorna had announced the pregnancy and Maddie was true to her word visited every day to help Lorna with the chores. She had taken great delight in helping to create the nursery and promised to be on hand whenever they wished to babysit. Life was going well for all of them so when they found Bertha on their doorstep in tears one morning it was a bit of a shock.

Apparently she had been woken early that morning by someone shaking her awake but when she finally opened her eyes there was no-one there and her husband Fred was sound asleep beside her, or so she thought. She tried to wake him but instead discovered he wasn't breathing, she called an ambulance and when they arrived they told her that he had passed away. She had just got back from the hospital where it was revealed that he had sustained a massive heart attack and died in his sleep. They reassured her that he wouldn't have felt a thing.

She felt she had nowhere else to go as they never had children of their own and she looked upon Lorna, Harry and Maddie as her own and therefore had wandered over to their place looking for a friendly shoulder to cry on.

Lorna and Harry were shocked to the core as Fred had always been an active man and despite the odd brandy was in their opinion a healthy man. Harry took Bertha's hand into his own, closed his eyes and tried to connect with Fred to no avail. This upset Bertha even more but Harry explained that sometimes it was difficult for newly passed people to have the energy to come through but he didn't have any doubt that he would at some point in the near future.

Bertha stayed with them for a few days as she couldn't face going back home with all the memories and Harry went to fetch her cats so they wouldn't be left alone. Irene very kindly offered to run the cafe until Bertha felt up to going back and she was amazed at the amount of flowers and offers of help that came through the door from her long established customers.

The funeral was a very distraught affair for Bertha and she lent heavily on Lorna & Harry for support. The service was very touching and the vicar delivered a beautiful sermon with some humorous anecdotes which brought about some laughter to lighten the atmosphere.

A small reception was held at the cafe afterwards for their close friends and once everyone had left Harry stayed behind to help Bertha clear up. It was then that Bertha took Harry to one side wishing to speak to him.

"What's up Bertha?" he asked.

"I have been doing a lot of thinking this past week" replied Bertha "And I have a proposition for you that I hope you and Lorna will accept. You know I consider you both as family especially as I don't have any children of my own don't you?"

"Of course, Bertha, we will always be here for you. You have been so good to us in the past there is no hesitation that we would look after you in your hour of need" said Harry.

"I know my dear, but what I want to say is that I am finding the cafe a bit too much to cope with on my own and with Fred gone my heart just isn't in it anymore" Bertha continued. "What I would like to do is to sign over the cafe to you with me just serving in it as I used to but without the hassle of running it, if that is o.k with you?"

"Oh my goodness, are you sure?" exclaimed Harry. "I will need to speak with Lorna but I'm sure that will be o.k but you can't just give it to us we should pay you for it".

"Most definitely not, I wouldn't hear of such a thing, besides it was left to you in my will in any case" replied Bertha. "You would be doing me a huge favour and it would take a great weight off my mind".

"Well I don't know what to say" exclaimed Harry. "I always thought that you had some nieces or nephews somewhere that you would leave the business to".

"I'm afraid not, both Fred and myself were only children and we don't know of any other family from our parents sides, you are the only family we have and that's why we have both said that if anything happened to us it should be left to you" explained Bertha. "So please say you will accept it, it would mean so much to me and I will rest easy knowing that you will be financially stable for the rest of your lives".

"Well if you put it like that, how can we refuse" replied Harry with a twinkle in his eye. "We won't know how to thank you though, words of appreciation do not seem enough somehow".

Bertha reassured Harry that a simple thank you would suffice and nothing would give her more pleasure and peace than knowing that she has helped them make a secure future for themselves. They meant so much to her and was concerned for their future especially with a little one on the way.

Lorna was equally amazed when Harry arrived home and relayed the news, she objected at such a huge gift at first but when Harry explained what it meant to Bertha for them to accept this she resigned herself to the idea and made a promise to herself that she would do everything in her power to make Bertha's life as comfortable as possible.

It was this in mind that they both visited the local market the following day and purchased the biggest bunch of roses, being Bertha's favourite flowers that they could afford and popped over to the cafe to deliver them.

Bertha was overcome with emotion at such a gesture and immediately started to hunt for several vases in which to place them. Her grief over losing Fred was still quite raw and such a kind thought had brought a fresh load of tears to her eyes. Lorna saw this and gave her a huge hug at which point Bertha collapsed into her arms with huge ranking sobs.

"Well we wouldn't have bought them if you were going to be upset" said Lorna trying to lighten the situation and make her smile but knowing all too well what she must be going through.

"Oh don't take no notice of silly old me" sniffed Bertha dabbing at her eyes with her laced edged apron.

"You will never be old or silly" interjected Harry who had been watching the scene and becoming concerned about Bertha's unhappiness.

It was at that point that he heard Fred's voice in his ear to tell Bertha that he was here with her and not to mess up that pinny that he had got her for her last birthday.

Bertha gasped when he relayed the message and grabbed Harry by the arm and with an almighty grateful hug told him that she now believed him to be here with her as no-one else knew that he had bought the apron for her.

Harry held both her hands in his at that point and sat her down, closed his eyes and in his mind asked Fred to come through again. He felt that the energy was quite weak which was only to be expected and to his surprise a young boy who had come through before brought Fred back.

The young lad said his name was Tim and he was the baby that Lorna had lost. He was glad they now knew who he was and he told Harry that whilst he wished he could be with them in the flesh he had more important work to do there. One of those tasks was to help Fred come through and he was chuffed to bits that he had finally managed it.

Tears were streaming down Harry's face at this point and both Bertha and Lorna were quite worried as to what was going on. However, when Harry explained what he had been experiencing they all ended up in floods of tears. Fred relayed some further reassuring words of comfort to Bertha and then Tim wanted to speak to his Mum. Harry held Lorna's hands which seemed to make the energy stronger and told Lorna that Tim was always going to be with her and whenever she saw a blue butterfly that would be him paying a visit.

The energy faded then and both Tim and Fred withdrew but there seemed to be a great atmosphere of peace within the cafe and they all knew that whatever happened their lost loved ones would always be with them and looking out for them from the other side.

Bertha seemed more restful when they finally left later that day and both Harry and Lorna hoped that the visit would now provide the closure that she so desperately needed. They couldn't wait to get back home and tell everyone what had transpired that day so they went immediately to Irene and Bill's to await Maddie coming home from school.

Maddie burst in a short time later full of eager chatter about what she had learnt and the latest gossip from Daisy. She was surprised to see her sister there but wasn't worried as they both looked so happy.

Once they had relayed the story of the day's events Maddie was eager to know if Tim knew about her. Harry assured her that he did indeed and that he was watching over all of them and he was sure that one of his duties would be that of a guardian angel for the new baby. With that Lorna let out a gasp as if Harry's comment was acknowledged by the small life inside her to confirm that this was indeed the case.

Maddie squealed with delight and rushed over to Lorna to give her belly a reassuring stroke and whispered to it that Tim was going to look after her.

"What makes you so sure it is a her" asked Lorna.

"Cos, I just do, you wait and see" replied Maddie full of confidence that she was right.

"We had better start choosing some girls names then" laughed Harry giving Maddie a knowing wink.

The due date was not for a few weeks yet so they both felt they had time to settle on a choice for both boys and girls names but they both had their personal choices. Harry quite liked Chloe for a girl and Joseph for a boy. Lorna wanted Rebecca or Daniel. They finally decided that if it was a girl then it would be Chloe Rebecca Weston or if a boy Daniel Joseph Weston. That way it pleased both of them.

The nursery was just about finished and they had had great fun furnishing it with beautiful fabrics and Harry had been busy painting the cot and cupboards a lovely bright sunshine yellow. Irene had made some pretty curtains for the window and Maddie had donated her favourite teddy which she lovingly placed in the finished cot. Everything was ready for the new arrival and by the beginning of March Lorna was feeling quite uncomfortable in the warm spring weather. Maddie insisted that she relax in the garden and put her feet up. She supplied her with endless glasses of homemade lemonade and Lorna felt quite spoilt and pampered. She was worried that she was keeping Maddie from her schoolwork but was assured that everything was in hand and not to worry. Maddie was very mature for her age and Lorna couldn't thank her enough for all the help she was providing.

Her assistance proved invaluable a couple of weeks later when again Maddie had popped round after school to find Lorna on all fours in the front room. Harry was over at the church doing some readings and was not due back for an hour or so.

"Whatever is the matter?" enquired Maddie getting somewhat nervous at the sight of her sister in such discomfort.

"I think your niece wants to make an appearance" gasped Lorna in between some strong contractions.

"Oh my goodness, what do you want me to do?" replied Maddie.

"Can you help me onto the settee please and grab some of those cushions for me" panted Lorna as another contraction gripped her swollen stomach.

Lorna was checking her watch and the contractions were coming thick and fast. She asked her sister to dash next door and get Mum and ask Bill to go and get Harry as she didn't think it was going to be long now.

Maddie was gone in an instant and it was only seconds later that Irene came bursting through the door armed with thick warm towels and barking orders to Maddie to go and put the kettle on. She reassured Lorna that Bill was on his way to collect Harry and that they wouldn't be long so just hang on in there.

"I don't think she wants to wait" said Lorna panting heavily now. Maddie was mopping her brow with a cool flannel and gripping her hand each time a new wave of contractions hit. "I need to push" she shouted just as her Mum came in with a bowl of warm water.

"Now you hold on there, my girl and we'll make you a bit more comfortable" replied Irene as she proceeded to place some warm towels under her. "How often are the contractions now?"

"About every three minutes" gasped Lorna. "Can I push yet?"

Just at that moment Harry burst through the door and went immediately to Lorna's side. Maddie gave him her hand and went round to the back of the settee and took hold of her other one.

"How is she doing?" asked Harry, quite worried now as Lorna didn't look too good.

"She'll be fine, I don't think it will be long now" replied Irene. "You just carry on holding her hand and I don't want no fainting now when the little mite makes an entrance, do you hear?"

Harry had no intention of missing one iota of the action but he was worried about Lorna and it gave him huge respect for the female race as to the obvious pain that they endured in order to prolong the human race.

Lorna's labour went on for another hour before her waters broke and the urge to push was even stronger. She couldn't stand it anymore and started to cry and it was only the sooth talking of her Mum that could console her.

Finally, at about 7.15 that evening baby Chloe Rebecca made her appearance into the world and with a healthy pair of lungs let out an extremely loud cry. Despite being a couple of weeks early she seemed completely healthy and the midwife that Bill had dashed out to get when he couldn't stand Lorna's suffering anymore confirmed as such. She was a healthy seven and a half pounds and after a quick check-up was cleaned up and handed to Harry. Lorna was extremely tired and after they had made her comfortable Harry brought their new daughter to her with tears in his eyes.

"My darling you are so beautiful and thank you so much for her and I'm so sorry that you had to go through so much pain" cried Harry as he handed the small bundle to Lorna.

"See I told you it would be a girl" said Maddie excitedly.

Lorna looked at her sister with so much love in her eyes and grasped her hand to say thank you for being here.

Irene, now satisfied that all was well insisted that everyone leave them to it for a while as they needed some alone time to become acquainted with their new child and she ushered them all out saying that they would pop back in an hour or so to see how things were.

The house fell silent with just the small gurgling's of the baby to be heard. Harry was in awe of Lorna who was now feeding Chloe and it seemed like the most natural thing in the world. He sent a silent prayer to heaven thanking them for all the blessings that had been bestowed on him over the past few years and vowed to continue his good work in helping others.

It was at that point when he heard a quiet giggle in his ear and he knew it was Tim who had been with them all this time and as if by confirmation a small blue butterfly landed on the coffee table, fluttered its wings three times and then flew back out of the open window.

CHAPTER TWENTY

The Weston households were filled with both the heavy scent of flowers and numerous visitors over the next couple of weeks. Maddie was in her element in helping to look after both the baby and Lorna so much so that on many occasions she slept the night on a spare put-you-up bed in the nursery.

Chloe was a contented baby and was soon gaining weight and she loved the teddy that Maddie had given her and would spend hours cooing at it as Maddie danced it about in front of her.

It wasn't long before Lorna and Harry were out and about taking long walks in the sunshine and showing off their pride and joy to anyone that they met along the way. One of their first visits was to Bertha at the cafe who was overjoyed to see them out and about. She had called on them at home in the early days but didn't want to intrude. They wanted to ask Bertha a favour and it was one that they hoped would give her immense pleasure.

"To what do I owe this lovely pleasure?" enquired Bertha as they came through the door. The cafe now belonged to Harry and Lorna and Bertha still refused to take any money for it and her only wish was to remain in the little flat above and live out the rest of her life in peace without the aggravation of running the business.

"Well, we would like to ask a favour" said Lorna not quite knowing where to start.

"Fire away deary" replied Bertha. "What can I do for you?"

Lorna looked sheepishly at Harry who took this as his cue to mention the favour to Bertha himself. After getting Bertha to sit at one of the unoccupied tables Harry broached the subject that they had called about.

"As you know I lost my Mum a number of years ago and I have considered you a surrogate Mum since I met you shortly afterwards" said Harry and he could see that this had brought a tear to Bertha's eyes. "Anyway we both feel that Chloe should have two grannies and we would feel very privileged if you would agree to being Nanny Bertha to her".

His request was met with silence and Harry could see from the tears streaming down Bertha's face that she would be honoured to be a replacement grandmother.

"You have no idea how happy that makes me" sobbed Bertha. "I never thought I would have a grandchild and I know it's not my own but it makes me feel so much part of your family and I feel that I shall never be alone again. You've made me a very happy woman".

"Then stop blubbing!!" laughed Lorna. "You'll only start your grand-daughter off".

With that Chloe awoke and started to cry so Lorna gently picked her up and placed her in Bertha's arms whereby she immediately settled down and back to sleep.

"It seems you are a natural, how much do you charge to baby-sit" asked Harry giving Bertha a wink.

"Absolutely no charge whatsoever" replied Bertha. "You have fully settled any childcare costs by giving me such an honourable position in your family. Now how about a nice cuppa and a large slice of homemade chocolate cake to celebrate?"

"Where on earth did you get chocolate from?" asked Lorna knowing all too well that the availability of chocolate was very scarce due to the severe rationing that they all endured.

Bertha went on to explain that Cadbury's had advertised that children should be allowed extra rations and she had applied to the authorities for an extra allowance due to the youngsters that visited her cafe. This was granted on the basis that it was sold to children and Bertha was quite happy to bend the rules slightly with a view to Maddie and Chloe benefiting from it.

They ended up spending the rest of the afternoon at the cafe as their departure was continually delayed by customers coming in who knew them and wanting a cuddle with Chloe. Arrangements were also started for Chloe's christening which they wanted to hold at the church where Harry gave his readings. It meant a lot to him to have it there as he had built up a lot of lasting friendships and he wanted to involve them all in some way.

Lorna also wanted to ask her father and she broached the subject with her Mum as she didn't want any undue upset on such a special day. Irene was happy for her to contact him after all if it wasn't for such a generous gift from him all those months ago they would not have been living in such lovely homes right next door to each other now.

Arnold was delighted to be invited, he had made an unexpected visit to see them just after Chloe had been born but he still felt that he didn't deserve to have such a blessing as a grand-daughter despite Lorna's assurances otherwise.

The christening was planned for the third Sunday in April and everyone was looking forward to it. Bertha wanted to cater for the event herself at the cafe and so it was that the guest list grew and grew as the customers wanted to give their blessings too.

The church was packed with well-wishers and as Lorna & Harry arrived carrying Chloe in the most beautiful christening gown which had become somewhat of a family heirloom. Both Lorna and Maddie had been christened in it as had their Mum years before. It was made from the most delicate lace and satin with a beautiful bonnet from the softest hand-made lace you could possibly wish for. They all made a very striking family as they stood round the font with the sun streaming through the colourful stained glass window behind them.

Lorna and Harry had asked Maddie to be a Godmother along with Joe and Beth, Harry's old army chums that he had stayed in contact with and who visited on a regular basis when their work commitments allowed.

Joe and Beth had been over the moon to be asked and were determined to make the christening despite Beth being heavily pregnant with a little brother or sister for Molly. They had arrived just in time to see Lorna, Harry and Chloe arrive and much fuss was made of them all. They had planned on staying overnight and Irene and Bill were putting them up as Maddie wanted to stay in the nursery that night.

The service went beautifully and Frank led them all in some rousing hymns. Chloe cooed and gaga-ed the whole way through and was in no way perturbed when she was anointed with the water. They were just about to walk away from the font when the most beautiful blue butterfly flew gently down and landed on the front of Chloe's christening gown. This was the final proof that they all needed to show that Tim was with them that day and was looking out for his young charge and they knew that he would protect her like any older brother would. It made them all smile and both Harry and Lorna gave silent thanks to him.

The whole day was enjoyed by everyone and Chloe was a dream child through the whole proceedings. She didn't cry once and only grumbled a little when she got hungry and Lorna disappeared for a short while to feed her. She wasn't allowed to go for long though as everyone wanted to see and have a cuddle with Chloe and it was quite late before they got home that night and they were totally exhausted. There was a mountain of presents from all their family and friends but they just didn't have the energy to open them. They promised Maddie that she could help them the following morning after breakfast. Maddie was thrilled with this and it made it feel like Christmas.

It was during the night that Joe and Beth were talking, they had had such fun that day and they really envied Lorna and Harry the life they led. The countryside was beautiful and so much more relaxing than the life they led in London. They therefore agreed that as they had no family left in London there was nothing tying them to the city and they would love to move out and be nearer their friends.

Joe promised Beth that as soon as the baby was born they would look for something nearby as they were so impressed with the community spirit here that they were sure it was an excellent place to bring up a young family and it would be lovely for Molly to be friends with Maddie and Chloe.

It was with this in mind that they broached the subject at breakfast the next day and everyone was so excited at their decision and welcomed them with open arms. Beth's baby was due in about a month's time and Lorna loved the idea that Chloe could grow up with him or her.

They were all sad to see them leave later that day but also excited about the new baby for Beth and the prospects that they would soon be living closer to each other. They promised to stay in touch and let them know as soon as the baby was born. In the meantime, they would have a hunt for houses for them and hopefully they could find one that was suitable and close by.

After a tearful farewell Joe, Beth and Molly disappeared over the horizon and they all traipsed back indoors to finish opening the presents. They had received some beautiful gifts and Lorna was taken aback by the generosity of their friends and family. Bertha had given them a solid silver christening set which had been in her family for years and she had the christening cup engraved with Chloe's name and date of birth.

"It's to be kept in your family now" said Bertha. "It's quite valuable so I am hoping that it can become a family heirloom for you".

"Bertha, thank you so much but you shouldn't have, you've given us so much already" replied Lorna.

"Nonsense, it is rightfully hers as she is my granddaughter after all" said Bertha with a wry smile. "Please accept them as it would mean so much to me".

Lorna and Harry couldn't believe the never-ending generosity of this woman, it was such a shame that she didn't have any family of her own as she so deserved a brood of children, grandchildren and great grandchildren around her. It seems such a crime that someone so wonderful could be alone. They made a pledge there and then that Bertha would be involved in every step of Chloe's life for as long as she was with them and Lorna dreaded the thought of what she would do the day they finally lost her. She had been such a comfort to them in times of trouble and she knew that she had been a great support to her Mum and Bill whilst the war was raging and both her and Harry had been caught up in it. They couldn't thank her enough for all that she had done for the family.

Lorna tried to put such thoughts to the back of her mind and prayed that they would still have many years together and hoped that she would be around to see Chloe grow and get to know what a wonderful grand-mother she had.

It was mid-May when Harry received the news that Beth had given birth to a bouncing baby boy, everyone was thrilled and whilst they hadn't had much success in finding a nice home local to them as yet they were still hoping that something would turn up soon.

Joe advised Harry that they were planning a trip down over the summer and Irene insisted on giving them Maddie's room again if Maddie was happy to sleep in the nursery. Maddie jumped at the chance as she doted on Chloe and the help in looking after her was a tremendous help to Lorna.

All four of them turned up one summer's day in June and Maddie immediately took charge of Molly and her new little brother Mikey. Beth was a bit unsure at first but having seen how competent she was with Chloe she was soon comfortable in Maddie occupying them whilst they talked about the house move.

Maddie had brought out a few saucepans and wooden spoons which she gave to Molly to play with whilst she got them both a glass of lemonade. Molly took great delight in making a right din banging away with all her might. The strange thing was that Mikey didn't seem to be concerned about the noise unlike Chloe who had started to cry. Maddie asked Molly to stop for a bit and gave her one of her old dolls to play with. After settling Chloe back to sleep she approached Mikey's pram and found him awake and just kicking his legs quite happily. Maddie knelt down beside him and with unseen hands started to clap very loudly. Mikey didn't respond, it was if he hadn't heard a thing.

Maddie went through to the front room where Beth and Joe were still in deep talks with Lorna and Harry and with a gentle touch on Beth's arm asked her to come into the kitchen with her.

The next thing the others heard was Beth crying so they rushed through to find out what was wrong. Maddie explained to them what had happened and that she thought something was wrong with Mikey. Joe's heart sank when he realised that perhaps Mikey hadn't been born so perfect after all. They hadn't even considered the possibility that he couldn't hear as he always seemed to respond to them but that would seem because they were always facing him at the time.

Joe and Beth quickly gathered their things and rushed Mikey to the local hospital. Maddie said she would look after Molly and not to worry she was sure it was nothing. Lorna and Harry were distraught at the news and tried to console Maddie who felt very upset at bringing such bad news to them.

Joe and Beth arrived at the hospital and were immediately seen by the doctor who undertook no end of tests and the results were not good. It appeared that poor little Mikey had no hearing whatsoever and the doctor recommended that they think about a special institution for the deaf which would give him the best life possible.

Joe was outraged at such a suggestion, he had never believed in those places where children were shut away from the outside world and he believed that every child deserved a loving family home environment in which to grow. The doctor tried to explain what a hard time they would have if they kept him at home but Joe was having none of it, Mikey was his son and no matter how hard it would be he was going to have him at home with them. Beth was too distraught to make an opinion and she leaned heavily on Joe to make the right choice for them all.

They all returned to Harry's feeling really upset, they had no idea what the future had in store for them now and they really didn't know where to turn.

Harry suggested that they all go to church and pray for a miracle for Mikey's hearing to be restored to him. So they all trotted down there with Mikey in tow whilst Irene and Bill watched over the children.

They met Frank at the door who was surprised to see them and was shocked when he heard the news. He had met Joe and Beth briefly at Chloe's christening and he had liked them immediately, they seemed such a lovely family and it seemed like a crime that Mikey should be suffering in this way.

Frank suggested that they have a session with Belinda who had got Harry going all that time ago when he discovered that he had a gift for healing. He arranged for them to come back tomorrow evening when he knew that Belinda would be there and he will explain everything to her.

So they duly returned the following night and Belinda met them at the door and showed them to a quiet room out the back. Mikey was fast asleep and Beth was concerned that she would need him to be awake but he had been fractious all day and she didn't want to wake him. Belinda assured her that it was not imperative that he was conscious and asked her to lay him in his blanket on the table with his head pointing towards her.

She then very carefully cradled his small head in her hands and with her thumbs pressed gently against his earlobes closed her eyes to concentrate. She seemed to stay in this position for what seemed like an age and when she finally released Mikey's head and opened her eyes she smiled at Joe and Beth and told them what she had seen.

"I can confirm that your son is indeed deaf in both ears, can I ask was it a normal delivery?" asked Belinda.

"Yes, but when he arrived he had the cord wrapped round his neck but they gave him a full check up and said he was fine" replied Beth.

"Ahh that would explain a lot" said Belinda. "It has been known that if there has been an interruption in the oxygen supply then this can affect the cochlea which is basically the part that is responsible for hearing".

"Can anything be done to help" asked Joe somewhat worried that his little boys hearing could not be restored.

"Unfortunately, there is no surgery that can rectify this but the good news is that I think with continued healing we can increase the energy in this area and hopefully this will reactivate the cochlea into responding to sound again and ultimately restore his hearing" advised Belinda.

"It may be a long laborious process and I cannot guarantee the end result but I am happy to try it if you are willing" she continued.

"Will it cause him any pain?" asked Beth concerned that her little boy would suffer with this process.

"He shouldn't feel a thing as I plan to undertake the healing whilst he is asleep as this is the best time for the body to enhance its natural healing ability" replied Belinda. "I understand that you don't currently live in this area?"

"Not at the moment, but we are looking to move as soon as possible" replied Joe.

"I'm sure Mum will let you stay with her for a while longer under the circumstances, Maddie can stay with us" said Lorna.

"May I suggest that you take up that offer because as soon as I can start the process on Mikey the better" informed Belinda.

"What about Molly and her schooling?" asked Beth.

"That's not a problem we can get her enrolled into Maddie's old school, it's only down the road from us and she would be going there anyway once you move" said Lorna.

The arrangements were therefore made and treatment was soon started to help Mikey. Belinda also had Harry present in order to teach him what to do so that he could give some healing when Belinda wasn't available.

The doctors were sceptical as to the usefulness of this treatment and still insisted that their best course of action would be to place Mikey in a special school. Both Joe and Beth were dead against this course of action and flatly refused to leave their beloved son in such an environment. Even if the healing that Belinda and Harry were giving didn't work they were determined to do the best that they could for their son and keep him at home. They had great faith and believed that they were sent this child for a reason and to pass him off to unknown authorities was not what was expected of them.

No matter how long it took they knew that one day Mikey would recover and it was that belief that they both clung to now.

CHAPTER TWENTY ONE

Joe returned home to pack up their house whilst Beth stayed behind with the children. Irene insisted that they stay with them as it would be more settling for Molly what with the new school and making new friends. In the meantime, Harry was scouting around for a suitable house for them to rent and a new job for Joe. Bill said that they may possibly have something at the coal merchants and would make enquiries.

So it was that a couple of weeks later both Harry and Bill had come up trumps on both fronts, Harry had found a small two up, two down little cottage on the other side of the village. It was in need of some repair but nothing that they couldn't manage between them and it was considerably cheaper than what they were paying in London. Harry took him over to see it the next weekend with Beth whilst the girls looked after the children and they were both excited and overjoyed at how quaint it was. Yes, it certainly needed some tender loving care but they all could see the potential in it and the landlord had given them carte blanch to do whatever they wished.

They immediately made plans to move in and commence redecoration and improvements whilst they were in situ. The cottage was set down a lovely little lane not too dissimilar to Harry & Lorna's and it had a pretty front garden which whilst overgrown would be lovely for the children to play in. Lorna offered with Irene's help to clear it and when they had done it they found some lovely old roses and shrubs which had been concealed by the long grass.

As promised Bill had enquired about a job at the coal merchants unfortunately nothing was available at the moment which led Bill to a serious discussion with Irene. He was fast approaching the time to retire and enjoy his life with Irene and felt that if he offered to train Joe up he could take over from him in a few months. Joe obviously wouldn't earn an awful lot in the meantime but with the substantially reduced rent he would now be paying they might just be able to manage. Irene thought this to be a marvellous idea and suggested to Bill that he broach the subject with his employers. This Bill duly did and they were more than happy to go along with the idea and agreed to pay Joe a small wage until he took over.

Joe called over the following Friday evening as he had been doing whilst Beth and the children had been staying there and Bill was anxious to tell him the news. They were both overjoyed at their good fortune and not only finding a nice place to live but to have a job to come to also. Bill was a bit concerned about the drop in wage for Joe but Joe reassured him that it was fine as together with the reduced rent they had a small amount in savings that would see them through.

This called for a big celebration so Irene prepared a sumptuous meal for them all for the following day which due to the fine weather they were able to enjoy outside in the garden where they could watch the children play under the expert guidance of Maddie.

Mikey was happily lying on a blanket in the warm sunshine, he had been receiving healing from Belinda every other day and whilst there did not appear any change Lorna thought he somehow looked more alert. Harry was due to undertake the first session with Belinda later that day when she finished her stint at the church, he was a bit apprehensive about it as he didn't want to ruin all the good that may have been done so far. Belinda assured him that that wouldn't happen and that any healing no matter how strong would be good for Mikey. Both Joe and Beth had every confidence in them both and they were still praying that the treatment would eventually work.

Mikey finally fell asleep just before Belinda arrived which was very fortunate as Belinda had said that this would be the most optimum time to treat him. They gently carried him upstairs to the bedroom and laid him on a large cushion on the floor. Belinda directed Harry as to how to hold his head and where to place each of his fingers and thumbs. In the meantime Belinda gently placed her hands from the front and facing Harry onto Mikey's shoulders. They both then went into a quiet meditative state and Harry could feel the heat emanating from his hands. They stayed there for a full ten minutes before Mikey began to stir and then wriggle from their grasp. He then let out a loud cry whereupon Harry picked him up to comfort him and walked him slowly back downstairs where Beth was waiting.

He was soon comforted once Beth had fed him and then they all joined the others back outside. Belinda congratulated Harry on his attempts and said he had given some good strong healing which she had felt being transmitted through her own hands. She had no doubt that Harry's ability was strong enough to take forward future sessions and hopefully in time will be of great benefit to the little chap.

Joe and Beth were feeling very fortunate to have Harry and Lorna as friends as not only were they helping their son but that had been instrumental in finding both a house and job for them so that they could move away from the grime of London. They were due to move into their new home the following week and Joe was to start his new job a few days later. They had all been busy undertaking renovations on the cottage and with some minor repair jobs, a lick of paint and new curtains and covers it was starting to look like home. Lorna and Irene had worked miracles with the gardens both front and back and Joe and Beth couldn't thank them enough. They agreed to invite them all round for dinner once they had moved in as a thank you for all their hard work. Harry & Lorna were over the moon to have them so close, their friendship had gone from strength to strength and they now considered them as family.

The move went very smoothly, Bill was able to borrow a lorry from work to transport everything down from London and with Harry and some neighbours help they managed to get everything into the new house by the end of the day. Maddie had complete charge of the little ones whilst Beth, Lorna & Irene cleaned and sorted the furniture as it came in. It wasn't long before everything was in its rightful place and was looking very cosy. Bertha came over with a huge picnic basket of goodies as a new home gift and they all sat down for a much needed rest and refuel.

Joe and Beth couldn't thank them all enough and were extremely grateful for everything everyone had done for them. They considered themselves very fortunate to have such close friends which seemed a bit strange to them at first as with all the years they had lived in London they had never built up such a relationship with anyone there.

"Well that will be country life for you" said Bertha. "We always look out for our own".

"Either that or we are just too damn nosey!" laughed Harry in response.

"Either way, we are just so glad to be here and you can be as nosey as you like" replied Joe. "We consider ourselves very fortunate to have such good friends around us, I don't know how we would have coped with everything that has happened if it hadn't been for you guys".

"You're entirely welcome!" chorused everyone together which brought about wails of laughter.

They spent the rest of the day just enjoying each other's company and apart from the short time that Harry took Mikey upstairs for some treatment they spent it together discussing everything and anything.

Harry was feeling quite confident now with Mikey and it was on one of his regular visits at the beginning of August after a session with him that something extraordinary happened. Harry didn't want to say anything to anyone until he had spoken to Belinda the following day when she was due to join him with the treatment.

When she finally arrived that afternoon Harry couldn't rush her upstairs quick enough on the pretence that he felt Mikey had been asleep for a while and was worried he would wake up before they could start any healing.

"Whatever's the matter?" asked Belinda as she was almost pushed through the bedroom door.

"I think the healing is working but I didn't want to say anything in case it was just my imagination" replied Harry.

"Why what happened?" asked Belinda really curious now as to what had occurred.

"Well yesterday when I finished Mikey woke up and I said to him "All done Mikey" but as I was still behind him he couldn't have seen my face but I swear he tipped his head up to look at me as if he had heard what I had said to him".

"Okay let's see what happens today" said Belinda as they both laid their hands on him.

It wasn't long before Mikey began to stir and they propped him up with some pillows and with both of them behind him, they clapped loudly in unison. The response was amazing, not only did Mikey turn his head to the sound but he went and clapped his own tiny hands together.

"Oh my goodness!" said Belinda. "I do believe we have finally cracked it Harry".

Belinda went on to do a couple of more tests using Mikey's favourite teddy which happened to have a squeak built in when you pressed its tummy. On both occasions Mikey turned towards the sound and giggled.

Harry couldn't contain his excitement anymore and went dashing to the top of the stairs and shouted for Joe and Beth to come up. They both came up the stairs taking them two at a time and burst through the bedroom door eager to know what had happened.

Harry showed them what Belinda had just demonstrated and Beth dissolved into a flood of tears and with tears also in Joe's eyes he went to give Harry and Belinda in turn the biggest bear hug he could manage. Words were not necessary at this point as everyone knew that a miracle had just occurred and Harry and Belinda had changed their son's life forever.

Belinda went on to explain that they mustn't get complacent about the achievements that had just occurred and it would be wise to take Mikey to the doctors to have him checked out. It would also be a good idea to continue with the healing for the time being at least until they were sure that his learning and especially his speech were in line with his age.

However, both Joe and Beth were in no doubt that all was now well and whilst they agreed to do as suggested they were in seventh heaven and couldn't wait to take him downstairs to tell the others of the good news.

After thanking everyone for everything that they had done for them Beth turned to Maddie and with tears in her eyes said,

"How can I ever thank you enough Maddie for without you spotting this so early it wouldn't have given Belinda the opportunity of putting it right so soon. She told me that as he was so young the healing had more of a benefit before he grew too much. Whereupon if it was left later the healing would not have had such a great outcome. So thank you and you are gonna get one hell of a birthday present from us this year" Beth added with a smile and a hug for her friend's sister.

Maddie was chuffed to bits to know that it was down to her that she had discovered Mikey's condition especially as she had been so afraid to voice her concerns originally. She also realised that Harry and Belinda had done a great job and she was so proud of her brother-in-law.

"Well they say things come in three's!" quoted Bertha as she gave Beth and Joe a comforting hug. "First the house, then the new job and finally Mikey recovering his hearing. I think that is cause for another celebration. How about everyone coming over to the cafe tomorrow and I'll lay on a party. You can invite whoever you want".

So that's what happened and most of their close neighbours attended as they wanted to pass on their best wishes after hearing the good news. Beth and Joe had made some more firm friends amongst them since they helped them move in and Beth and Joe felt truly loved within the community.

The following week they took Mikey to see the doctor and after viewing the previous records was astounded as to the result of the healing. He congratulated them on the success they had seen and called it nothing short of a miracle. Harry continued to give Mikey treatment and each session showed promise and it wasn't soon before Mikey was babbling away to himself obviously in awe of hearing his own voice. Beth and Joe would sit and listen to him for hours and Molly doted on him. She was only five years old but insisted on helping out with anything that involved him.

The day of Maddie's 13th birthday dawned bright and sunny and the Weston household was woken early by her to the shriek of wrapping paper being torn. She was now a teenager and she seemed to have suddenly grown up overnight. She had wanted to stay the night at Lorna's but Lorna insisted that she should be with her Mum knowing all too well what presents awaited her and the noise that that would create at such an early hour. However, she promised they would all come round once she had got Chloe dressed and fed.

Maddie was beside herself with excitement, her friend Daisy was coming round later and they were all going to see "Make Mine Music" at their local picture house which was a Walt Disney film that had been released earlier that year. Neither of them had been to see a movie before and they were both very excited but none more so when there was a knock on the door about 9 o'clock and she opened it to find Beth, Joe, Molly and Mikey standing there with a brand spanking new bicycle all wrapped up with a huge red ribbon.

"Well we did promise" said Joe with a huge grin as he took in Maddie's completely shocked face.

"Oh my goodness, is that all for me?" she shrieked. She had never had anything so new before and her old bike had seen better days.

"It most certainly is" replied Beth "And you totally deserve it you wonderful young lady. Besides every teenage should have a good bicycle" she continued giving Maddie a hug.

"Thank you, thank you, thank you, I never expected anything like this" cried Maddie as she hugged them all back and then started to remove the ribbon so she could ride it straight away.

"Hang on there, isn't it better you get dressed first before you go pedalling off in your nightgown" said Irene who had come to the door to see what the commotion was about. She knew about the bike of course as Beth had checked with her that it would be alright to get it. Irene was happy for them to do that but only if they could really afford it as she knew that Joe was still on a reduced wage and would be until the end of the year when Bill retired. She was assured though that it was fine and they had promised Maddie earlier that month and had a new bike in mind then.

Harry, Lorna and Chloe turned up at that point and they all went inside to have a birthday breakfast. No sooner had they finished and cleared up there was a knock on the door and Daisy stood there with a huge brightly wrapped box in her hands. Her mum Trish was with her and was carrying a smaller present but wrapped in the same brightly coloured paper. Maddie almost pulled Daisy off her feet as she dragged her inside to show her her new bike and as Daisy admired it Maddie carefully opened the present from her. It was a beautiful party dress which Trish had spent many weeks making and the colour was the most gorgeous soft lilac that Maddie had ever seen. She begged her Mum to be able to wear it when they went out which she agreed but told her that she would have to change if they were going out later to ride their bikes. The small package from Trish was the most delicate silver bracelet with tiny amethyst beads woven within the links of the chain and matched the dress perfectly.

Bertha also arrived later with the biggest birthday cake Maddie had ever seen with her name and 'Happy 13th Birthday' written across the middle in the most beautiful lilac writing. Irene invited her to stay for tea later when the girls came back from the film so that they could celebrate as a whole family. Bertha became very emotional and she thanked them all for taking her into their family and their hearts and could think of no better place to be.

Maddie was beside herself with joy at how spoilt she was and went round giving everyone a big hug. This was the best birthday EVER!!!

So it was that their lives continued on an even keel, Mikey grew up and started school with no hint of his earlier deafness, Molly grew into a beautiful young girl who still to this day dotes on her brother and they all still live in the little house across the village from the Weston's.

Bill retired at the end of the year as planned and Joe took over his job and was doing very well. Irene was also taking it a bit easier as the hard life she had previously led was now taking its toll so they spent a lot of time relaxing and taking long walks in the country side around their home.

Lorna's Dad Arnold married Sue and they had a happy life together. Frank and Belinda remained close family friends and continued to give help and guidance to Harry.

Bertha remained Chloe's 'grandmother' and she doted on her always until she passed away at the ripe old age of 92. She was sorely missed by everyone and left a huge void in everyone's heart. Harry had several messages from her in subsequent years and they all knew she was happy after being reunited with her beloved Fred and they knew she would always be with them in their hearts.

As for Lorna and Harry they went on to have two more children, a little boy who they named Tim in honour of Chloe's guardian angel and another little girl they called Rebecca but soon was to become Becci as Chloe thought it a nicer name.

Chloe grew up and was very close to Mikey and they all often played together and were always there to support one another as they grew up and experiencing all the trials and tribulations that childhood brings along with celebrating with them all the joys too.

Harry started his own healing practice under the guidance of Belinda and he continued with his readings supported by Frank. He was doing very well and after a few years they were able to move to a larger house that could support their growing family.

Maddie became a beautiful young lady who was sought after by all the eligible bachelors in the village. She became a primary school teacher in the school where she herself was taught and ended up teaching her two young nieces and nephews.

Lorna became a pillar of the community and was well loved and respected by all who knew her. She raised a beautiful family and was adored by Harry. They had a long and happy marriage and she went on to become a proud grandmother to 10 grandchildren all of whom adored her also. Both Harry and herself received British Campaign Medals for their work during the war and with all that conflict behind them they too settled into a happy and contented life. Lorna's War was over and peacetime reigned in the fullest sense of the word.

THE END

Lightning Source UK Ltd.
Milton Keynes UK
UKHW010719190720
366728UK00001B/39